"You're not my conscience."

"I don't think you have one," Cassie said coldly. "Do you want to get married, Mr. Gilmour, or do you enjoy playing the field?"

The question popped out before she could help it, and she lowered her eyes, waiting for him to tell her it was none of her business.

"I'd be a liar if I said I didn't enjoy dating beautiful women," he admitted. "Though lately I've found it equally enjoyable staying home with a good book. I mean it," he added as she glanced up at him. "So, either I need to recharge my batteries or widen my female circle."

"Or settle down with the right woman."

Wide shoulders lifted in a shrug. "I've a low threshold of boredom, Cassie, and I've yet to meet the girl who excites me the *whole* time."

"How tedious to be excited the *whole* time," she retorted.

ROBERTA LEIGH wrote her first book at the age of nineteen and since then has written more than seventy romance novels, as well as many books and film series for children. She has also been an editor of a woman's magazine and produced a teen magazine, but writing romance fiction remains one of her greatest joys. She lives in Hampstead, London, and has one son.

Books by Roberta Leigh

ROBERTA LEIGH

Two-faced Woman

Harlequin Books

TORONTO • NEW YORK • LONDON
AMSTERDAM • PARIS • SYDNEY • HAMBURG
STOCKHOLM • ATHENS • TOKYO • MILAN
MADRID • WARSAW • BUDAPEST • AUCKLAND

Harlequin Presents first edition March 1993
ISBN 0-373-11541-5

Original hardcover edition published in 1991
by Mills & Boon Limited

TWO-FACED WOMAN

CHAPTER ONE

CASSIE ELLIOT stepped out of the taxi and stared at the imposing marble and glass headquarters of Barlow Publishing which dominated one corner of Hanover Square.

Unbelievable to think she was the new owner.

Even more unbelievable was that she had never met the man who, until his death three months ago, had controlled this prestigious publishing empire. Indeed she had been unaware of his existence until his lawyer, Lionel Newman, had come to the Park Avenue penthouse in New York, where she lived with her mother and stepfather, to inform her she was Henry Barlow's daughter and sole heir.

'I thought my father died soon after I was born!' she had exclaimed, glancing from the urbane Englishman standing in front of her to her mother, seated opposite on a pale apricot silk couch.

'As far as I was concerned he did,' her mother said staunchly. 'From the moment you were born he had no time for us.'

Lionel Newman gave an embarrassed cough. 'Henry was always a workaholic. His entire life revolved round the books he published and their authors.'

'The only reason he married me was because he wanted a son to succeed him,' Margaret Elliot explained to her daughter. 'When the specialist informed him I couldn't have any more children he asked for a divorce. I assumed it was because he wanted to remarry and try again, but if he left everything to you I guess he remained single.'

'Quite so,' the lawyer added. 'Though he didn't maintain direct contact with you and your mother, Miss Barlow, he——'

'Miss Elliot,' Cassie intervened. 'I've taken my step-father's name.'

'I see. Well, as I was saying, he employed a detective agency to monitor your well-being, and always retained a sense of paternal duty towards you.'

'There's more to being paternal than leaving your child money,' Margaret Elliot stated, glancing round the exquisitely furnished living-room that overlooked the marble terrace. 'As you see, Cassie hasn't lived in poverty since Henry left me. My second husband, Luther Elliot, regards her as his daughter.'

This was true. Cassie adored her stepfather, and considered his three sons by his first marriage to be her brothers. Glancing at her mother, she was filled with love for her. As sweet-natured as she was beautiful, she devoted her time to a charitable foundation set up by her husband, and Cassie, after graduating from college, helped her.

But it didn't stretch her mentally, and for a long while she had been searching for something else to do. The trouble was, her history degree equipped her either for a teaching or research job, neither of which appealed.

The news this British lawyer had brought her seemed the ideal solution, though never in her wildest dreams had she envisaged owning and running a publishing house in a strange country. Even as it excited her it filled her with fear. But she had never been afraid of a challenge, and she was going to take it.

Lionel Newman was opposed to the idea when she told him. 'You have no business experience, Miss Bar—Miss Elliot, and Barlow's is a large company. Miles Gilmour—he's the managing director and senior editor—has run it successfully for ten years, and can raise the money to buy your shares.' The lawyer hesitated momentarily before continuing. 'As a matter of fact your late father proposed leaving Barlow's jointly to Mr Gilmour and yourself, but he died before he could sign his new will.'

Common sense told Cassie to let the man buy her out, but she was in the happy financial position of not having to be sensible, and intended learning how to run Barlow's herself.

Was she behaving like a spoiled little rich girl who had been given a new toy to play with? she asked herself now as she crossed Barlow Publishing's black and white tiled foyer, and went up in the lift to the top floor, which housed the executive suites. She was meeting Mr Gilmour and Lionel Newman at ten and, uncertain how long the journey from Claridge's would take in the rush-hour traffic, found she had forty minutes to spare. Still, it was better than keeping them waiting!

'I'm Miss Elliot,' she informed the young receptionist. 'I've an appointment with Mr Gilmour.'

'He's at a meeting, but should be through shortly. He said for you to wait in his office.' Clearly her name meant nothing to the girl, for she showed no curiosity. 'You'll enjoy it here,' she added as she led the way down a carpeted corridor to the outer office of the managing director's suite. 'That's if you get the job, of course. Mr Gilmour's seen four secretaries already, but no one as good as Mrs Darcy.'

Cassie hid a smile, understanding the receptionist's lack of curiosity about her. She assumed Cassie was applying for the job! 'What happened to Mrs Darcy?'

'She broke her hip, and there were lots of complications with it.' The girl pointed to a chair. 'Make yourself comfortable while you're waiting. If you need the cloakroom, it's the door opposite.'

Left alone, Cassie admired the honey-coloured carpet and sleek black furniture, the desk covered by the latest word processor and fax machine. Three contemporary paintings hung on the walls, and she wondered if they reflected Mr Gilmour's taste or an interior decorator's.

She glanced at her watch. Still thirty-five minutes until their appointment. Bored, she wandered into the cloakroom to check on her appearance. She had taken care to appear businesslike, and her navy Chanel suit and white silk blouse was the outfit to impress. Was it a little too obvious, perhaps? Anyway, she was stuck with it.

Yet what did she care what Mr Gilmour thought of her? She wasn't answerable to him, rather the other way round. Well, that wasn't strictly true, she admitted. For the moment, at least, he was the only person capable of running the company, and if he left, many of Barlow's authors would follow him.

'He understands how to handle their egos,' the lawyer had informed her. 'Most authors have to be pampered like film stars.'

It wasn't only the authors who appreciated him, though. Her stepfather had made discreet enquiries and learned he was greatly respected by his competitors, who would be more than happy to poach him. Cassie hoped his loyalty to her father's memory would extend to her, but if not, was prepared to offer him a financial inducement to stay on.

Leaving the cloakroom, she was on the threshold of the office when an incisive masculine voice, coming from Mr Gilmour's room, spoke her name.

'The hell with Catherine Barlow! There's no way I'll work for her. I find it hard to forgive Henry for putting me in such an invidious position.'

'It wasn't his intention, as you know,' came Lionel Newman's softer tones. 'It was unfortunate he had a heart attack before he could sign his new will.'

'Well, I've no intention of acting wet-nurse to a spoiled brat who fancies playing career woman until she gets bored with it. I've had three damn good offers—two here, and one in the States. My mind is made up, Lionel. If she's in, I'm out.'

'Meet her before you decide; for Henry's sake if nothing else,' the lawyer pleaded.

'I won't go until I've found a suitable replacement. That's all I'll promise. Dammit, Lionel! If she had a conscience she'd do as Henry had intended.'

Not waiting to hear more, Cassie retreated to the cloakroom to think over the position. It was impossible for her to run Barlow's on her own, nor could she learn how to do so without Mr Gilmour's help. She appreciated his anger, but didn't feel guilty for being left the shares. Indeed, knowing her genetic father had not planned on leaving her the entire business, she found it ironic that he had done so by default.

But default or not, her father had—without meaning to—provided her with a *purpose* in life, and since this was the only thing he had ever given her, she was going to keep the company until she had made up her mind whether or not she wanted to run it.

CHAPTER TWO

PURPOSEFULLY Cassie went down the corridor. She remembered seeing a public telephone as she had stepped out of the lift, and she checked to make sure she had change.

'Mr Gilmour just went into his office,' the receptionist said in surprise. 'Didn't you see him?'

'Yes. But he asked me to give him five minutes, and I want to make a phone call while I'm waiting.'

Dialling the number of Barlow's main switchboard, she asked to be put through to Mr Newman, who was in Mr Gilmour's office.

Within a moment the lawyer was on the line. 'Yes?' he enquired.

'Don't mention my name, Mr Newman, but this is Cassie Elliot, and I don't want Mr Gilmour to guess you're talking to me.'

'Carry on,' he said in an even tone.

'Will you please pretend this is your secretary calling to say Miss Barlow rang to cancel this morning's meeting with you and Mr Gilmour? A great friend of hers is unexpectedly getting married and she's flown back to the States for the wedding.'

The hesitation was momentary. 'Very well.'

'I'll call in at your office in about an hour to explain, if that's OK with you?'

'Yes, do that.'

Cassie couldn't help a chuckle at the dryness of his response. 'One other thing, Mr Newman. Does Mr Gilmour know I use the name Cassie Elliot, and not Catherine Barlow?'

'No.'

'You're positive—it's *very* important.'

'Absolutely positive. I'll see you shortly.'

On her way back to the office she passed the lawyer on his way out, but even though he must have been longing to question her, with true British phlegm he walked by as if he didn't know her.

Once again she went into the cloakroom, anxious to make herself look less expensively dressed. No secretary could afford a couture suit, and, while she wasn't sure if Mr Gilmour would recognise a Chanel if he saw one, it was too big a chance to take. Removing her jacket, she folded it so that the label was hidden, and took off all her chunky gold jewellery, except for her watch—it was a Rolex Oyster, but Far Eastern copies abounded and this could easily be mistaken for one, as could her leather quilted Chanel bag.

Inspecting herself in the mirror, she decided she would do. Above average in height, and beautifully proportioned, she had the colouring and features of a true brunette: lightly tanned skin, wide-apart sherry-brown eyes flecked with gold, which made them appear lighter; thick, tawny-brown hair, normally worn long and casual, but tucked into a neat chignon for today; a slightly tip-tilted nose, and a large, well-shaped mouth that added piquancy to her appearance.

Since graduating from college she had occasionally acted as a model at charity fashion shows, and had run the gamut of hundreds of pairs of eyes, both male and female. After an initial embarrassment, she had accepted the fact that firm, full breasts above a small waist, allied to long, shapely legs, attracted both admiration and envy—the former from men, the latter from women.

Brought up with three self-confident stepbrothers, Cassie had absorbed their attitude to life. But she had never had to test her mettle until now. Perhaps this was another reason why she wanted to find out if she had a business brain.

Drawing a deep breath, she left the cloakroom, knocked on the door of Mr Gilmour's office, and went in.

The size of the room and the size of the man impressed Cassie simultaneously, for both were large and imposing. Black suede armchairs and couches stood on thick, silver-grey carpet, and in front of the window stood a huge Art Deco desk of macassar wood and ivory, as sleek and polished as the man who rose from behind it.

Well over six feet, with the build of a footballer, powerful shoulders and chest tapered down to a trim waistline. She knew him to be thirty-four, but he appeared older. Lines etched the long narrow nose and firm, thin-lipped mouth, while grey eyes appeared lighter by being set beneath strong black brows. His hair was black, too, the front lightly sprinkled with grey, and springing back from a high forehead in an unruly wave. Dishy, she thought, and momentarily wished she was meeting him as her real self, and not embarking on a deception. But recalling the conversation she had overheard, the regret was fleeting.

'I'm Cassie Elliot,' she stated crisply. 'I understand you require a secretary?' Assuming an English accent was easy, influenced as she was by her mother's, which she had often mimicked. And if he did notice an American twang she had an answer ready.

'There's been a change of plan,' he replied, his voice sounding deeper now she was facing him. 'I only need someone for six months. So if you want a permanent position...'

'Not necessarily. I'm bored where I am, and fancy a change. Good secretaries are always in demand, and it won't be a problem finding another job.'

He nodded and sat down, motioning her to do the same. The light from the window shone full on his hair, and she noticed a hint of russet in it. That could account for his short manner. She'd take a bet he had a temper too.

'You sound confident of your ability,' he commented. 'I hope it's justified?'

'I think so,' she smiled. 'First, I should explain I didn't come from an agency. I heard from Mr Newman, my present employer, that you required a secretary, and decided to apply—with his approval, of course.'

Miles Gilmour frowned. 'I was with him a moment ago, and he didn't mention you. In fact his secretary called him here.'

'It was the new girl,' Cassie said, wishing she had had more time to prepare her story. 'I've been training her in.'

'I see. Well, I'm not *au fait* with Mr Newman's manner of working, but I should warn you I don't tolerate clock-watchers, lateness, or gossiping on the telephone.'

'I don't clock-watch or gossip, Mr Gilmour, as Mr Newman will confirm.' Her voice was firm. Much as she wanted this man to employ her, she refused to be treated like a slave. 'As to telephone calls—I occasionally receive and make them, but I keep them brief.'

'Then you're unique in the annals of women!' he said sourly. 'Tell me about yourself.'

'I'm twenty-four, and I've been with Mr Newman for two years.'

'I've never seen you in his office.'

Cassie took a chance. 'I shouldn't think you notice secretaries when you're at a meeting!'

'True,' he said without a smile. 'Where did you work before?'

'In Dublin.'

'That accounts for your accent. What brought you to London?'

'Family commitments,' she answered truthfully, relieved when he didn't pursue the matter.

'If you work for me there'll be some travel involved,' he went on. 'Will that present any problems?'

'Not at all—I enjoy travelling.'

'They won't be vacations. I don't mix business and pleasure.'

There was no mistaking his meaning, and she reddened, annoyed that he deemed it necessary to warn her. Did he think he was irresistible?

'I'm not short of boyfriends, Mr Gilmour. And anyway, you aren't my type.'

'Thank God for that!' Eyes narrowed, he contemplated her. 'I can see I won't be having a yes-woman working for me.'

'You mean I have the job?'

'Providing Lionel confirms you're as good as *you* think you are!' He reeled off salary and office hours, then rose to show the meeting was at an end. 'I'd like you to start as soon as possible.'

'I'll be free next Monday.'

'I can't wait a whole week. Make it the day after tomorrow.'

She was tempted to agree in case he found someone else who was prepared to start sooner, but with no secretarial skills whatever, she needed to learn the basics. 'I'm sorry, but I promised Mr Newman I——'

'All right,' he said testily. 'I'll manage somehow. I may not be able to talk to him until this afternoon. Leave your number, and I'll call you.'

'I'd rather phone *you*,' she replied hastily, and hurried away, intent on seeing the lawyer before Miles Gilmour contacted him.

As befitted his aura, Lionel Newman's offices were situated in a Georgian terrace house in Bedford Square, and judging from the number of partners listed on the board in the entrance hall it was a firm of considerable size.

'You've set my curiosity alight,' he greeted her as she was ushered in. 'What are you up to?'

Concisely Cassie explained, careful to state that she had not intentionally eavesdropped. 'I was going to interrupt and walk in when I heard Mr Gilmour tell you he was leaving the company. That's when I knew I had to find a way of ensuring he stays on to teach me what I want to know.'

Pale blue eyes locked with hers. 'If Miles had met you properly, as Catherine Barlow, he might have changed his mind about you.'

'I couldn't take that chance. He's so angry at the way things have turned out—understandably, of course—that he'd never have agreed to show me how to run the company.'

'He's hardly likely to show his secretary,' came the dry comment.

'Not intentionally,' Cassie acceded. 'But don't forget I'll be working closely with him, and it will give me a marvellous opportunity to study his methods.'

'You're putting me in a difficult position, Miss Elliot,' the lawyer murmured.

'Cassie, please.' She leaned forward, giving him the battery of sherry-gold eyes. 'I'm sorry I had to involve you, but it was all I could come up with. Please, Mr Newman,' she implored. 'For the sake of your friendship with my father, help me.'

He softened visibly, her natural warmth and charm impossible to resist when she turned both full on.

'There's one thing I'd like your assurance on first,' he said. 'That if you do decide to take over the running of the company you'll offer Miles a partnership. For the past ten years he's *been* the company, and it's the least he deserves.'

'Agreed—though I don't think he'd accept. But I'll give him a more than generous golden handshake if he goes.'

'Fair enough.' The lawyer leaned back in his chair, stroking his chin. 'This charade won't be easy for you, Cassie. You've never had to earn a living, and I can't see you taking orders.'

'It will be tough,' she admitted. 'But Mr Gilmour's the best person to teach me about publishing, so I'll stick it for as long as it takes.'

'So be it. Where will you live?'

'A good question, that. I can hardly remain at Claridge's! I'll find a small apartment—flat,' she corrected hastily. 'Nothing too smart, but not **too** gross either. Perhaps I'll pretend I have a small private income.'

'I'm sure you'll be able to work out the details—you clearly have a fertile mind!'

'I'll be needing it in the months to come!'

'Do you have any family or friends here?'

'A few distant cousins and a number of friends. I suppose I'd better give them a wide berth in case Mr Gilmour knows any of them.' She pulled a face. 'The ramifications of all this are beginning to come home to me.'

'Give it up, then.'

'Never!'

'Of course, you might grow to like Miles,' the lawyer said slyly. 'Your mother was your father's secretary before they married, you know, and history has a way of repeating itself.'

'It won't this time!' Cassie was appalled by the suggestion. Her future employer might be physically attractive but he was also boorish and bossy. 'He's already warned me against any romantic notions,' she added.

'A sensible precaution for a man so attractive and vulnerable.'

'Vulnerable as a tiger!' she snorted.

'Vulnerable as in bachelor!' came the reply. 'Miles is besieged by females.'

'This is one female who won't be besieging!' She changed the subject. 'I have one more favour to ask you. I need a quick course in office procedure, and I'd like to spend the next week here, learning.'

'I'll ask my secretary to help you. Is there anything else?'

'Could you tell Mr Gilmour that Catherine Barlow has changed her mind about coming over to learn the business, and will decide within six months what she wants to do. In the meantime she has instructed you to give him the authority to carry on as before.'

The lawyer half smiled. 'You've thought of everything, haven't you?'

'I'm sure I haven't,' she said ruefully. 'I've a feeling I'll be living on a knife-edge.'

'If it becomes too sharp you can always revert to being Catherine Barlow. And I must confess I wish you weren't going on with this. Miles will be very bitter when he learns the truth.'

'Not if he ends up a partner or walks away with a golden handshake.'

'Money isn't the be all and end all.'

'I know,' she replied. 'That's why I want to do something worthwhile with my life. And Barlow's is my solution.'

Driving back to Claridge's later that day, after spending the rest of it with Lionel Newman's secretary, Cassie experienced an unexpected pang at the thought of the father she had never known. What quirk in his character had made him reject her because she had been a girl and not a boy? She would probably never know. Her mother refused to discuss him, and Lionel Newman was less than forthcoming on the subject. Perhaps she might glean something from Miles Gilmour. He appeared to have been close to him, and had sounded hurt as much as angry with her father for not changing his will sooner.

Had it been a genuine mistake on Henry Barlow's part, or had he used the promise as a ploy to retain his protégés' loyalty? This was another question that would never be answered. But one thing *was* certain. Six months from now she hoped to assume the mantle of command, and if Miles Gilmour didn't wish to share it with her, he could leave.

At least she would give him an option, which was more than he had intended to give *her*.

CHAPTER THREE

FINDING somewhere to live was not as easy as Cassie had hoped, and after inspecting half a dozen flats within the limits of her salary, she soon abandoned the idea and decided to dip into her funds.

From her first glimpse of the freshly painted terrace house in Primrose Hill she knew she had found what she wanted. It had two small bedrooms and a large reception-room, and had recently been modernised and refurbished. In addition it had the added attraction of a prettily tiled patio at the rear and a parking bay in the front.

She moved in the next morning, and that afternoon shopped for clothes to suit her new working life, returning home laden with boxes and bags.

It was eight o'clock before she had put everything away, and realised she was ravenous. Not surprising when she hadn't eaten since breakfast. Too tired to shop for food, she slipped on a jacket and made for the little Greek restaurant she had noticed at the bottom of the road.

It was packed, and she had to wait twenty minutes before being shown to a table, but the meal when it came made the waiting worthwhile, and she tucked hungrily into a mini-feast.

Most of her fellow diners were of similar age to herself—given the cheapness and standard of the food, it was not surprising—and before long she was talking to the couple at the next table, which was almost touching hers. They introduced themselves as Pete and Julie Goodwin, and said they lived near by.

'I'm Cassie Elliot, and so do I!' she responded. 'In fact, I've just moved in.'

Over several cups of Turkish coffee Cassie learned that
Pete was an accountant, and his wife a doctor in a local
group practice.

'We're giving a party on Sunday,' Julie said as they
all rose to leave. 'Drop in if you're free. If you have a
boyfriend bring him along—if not, we guarantee you'll
have one before the evening's over!'

'I haven't anyone special so I'll come alone,' Cassie
smiled, and wrote down their address. 'What time?'

'Seven onwards, and dress is informal,' Pete said.

Slim and fair-haired, Pete appeared to be in his early
thirties, Julie a few years younger. She too was blonde
and slender, with neat features and pale skin, and they
could easily have passed for brother and sister. Their
clothes were casual yet expensive, marking them out as
upwardly mobile, and she wondered if they thought the
same about herself. She had meant to change into one
of her new, inexpensive outfits, but had felt too tired,
and was wearing a cherry-red Armani suit and royal blue
and red blouse.

Pleased to have made some friends, her spirits rose.
She was starting a new life in a totally alien world, but
at least she wouldn't be lonely. From what Julie and
Pete had said, they had a number of single friends of
both sexes, and if they were all as nice as them she would
be happy to be accepted into their circle.

On her return home she had an urge to speak to her
parents, and not wanting them to guess it was because
she was homesick, she pretended it was to give them her
new phone number and address.

'I don't like you living alone in a house,' her mother
protested. 'Couldn't you find an apartment?'

'I have a burglar alarm and friendly neighbours, so
stop fussing,' Cassie instructed good-naturedly. 'It's safer
here than New York.'

'How did your meeting with Gilmour go?' This from
her stepfather, who was listening on an extension.

Cassie filled him in, breathing a sigh of relief when
she heard him chuckle. Had Luther Elliot been against

her plan, she would have had serious doubts about continuing with it.

'I hope you can hang in there for as long as it takes you to get a working knowledge of Barlow's,' he said. 'Make notes of everything Gilmour does and tells you, and try to swot up on accountancy. The ability to read a balance sheet is a great asset.'

Cassie went to bed in a happier mood, and nine-thirty next morning found her sitting in the office of Miss Pike, Lionel Newman's secretary, trying to master the complexities of a word processor. Luckily she found it easy to follow the manual, and by the end of the day felt she wouldn't make a fool of herself when she had to cope alone. Unfortunately her typing was of the two-fingered variety, and her shorthand non existent, but these were two problems she knew how to deal with, and she did so during her lunch-break.

First she visited a typing bureau which Miss Pike had recommended, then took a taxi to a shop in Oxford Street, where she bought the tiniest micro recorder available. Then, considerably happier, she returned to the office.

The Goodwins' party on Sunday was fun, and Cassie swapped telephone numbers with a couple of girls of her own age. She was more careful with the men. In spite of attracting a fair number to her side, none particularly interested her until the evening was halfway through, when a late arrival caught her eye.

As he entered the crowded room, his gaze ranged slowly over her, making her aware of every curve she had, and it was not long before he edged his way towards her.

'I haven't seen you at the Goodwins' before,' he said. 'Are you a long-lost relative?'

'A new-found friend,' she smiled.

'I hope you'll be one of mine too! I'm Justin Tyler. I'm a colleague of Julie's.'

'How many partners do you have in the practice?' she asked, after introducing herself.

'Five, and we all have different specialities. Mine's paediatrics.'

Cassie couldn't envisage him as a baby-doctor. Tall and slim, with sandy-brown hair and light blue eyes, he looked like an advertising executive or stockbroker. He had a nice sense of humour and was easy to talk to, and before long she was telling him about her new job, disconcerted to discover he knew Miles Gilmour.

'We were at Oxford together,' he explained. 'He got a First, of course.'

'Why "of course"?' she couldn't help asking.

'Because he was so bloody clever! It gave him an air of superiority that he's never lost.'

'I can't say I've noticed it. He has a good opinion of himself, and he's forthright, but then, most successful men are.'

'I dare say I'm prejudiced,' Justin confessed. 'We were never great friends. In fact we've only stayed in touch because of my sister and her husband.'

He did not volunteer any further information, but mention of his sister made Cassie wonder what type of female appealed to her new employer.

'How about having dinner with me one night this week?' Justin broke into her thoughts.

'Sounds lovely,' she said. 'Name the evening. At the moment I've an empty diary.'

'A girl as beautiful as you!'

'I'm new to the big city.'

'Where do you hail from?'

Wishing she could be truthful, Cassie named Cheltenham, the town where her mother's cousins lived, and was relieved when their conversation was interrupted by another couple joining them, though not before Justin had arranged to see her on Wednesday.

'It's my day off, so I won't be tired,' he informed her. 'I'd hate to doze off on our first date!'

Cassie doubted this had ever happened. Industrious and dedicated he might be, but she was positive he played with as much enthusiasm as he worked.

By the following morning the only thought in her head was the task ahead of her, and, gloomily hoping the blustery summer day didn't presage her relationship with her new employer, she donned one of her 'working outfits'—a tailored navy silk suit with crisp emerald-green blouse—and presented herself in his office.

He was standing by his desk, flinging things into a bulging black leather briefcase.

'Sorry about this,' he greeted her, 'but I have to go to Cork to see Seamus O'Mara. His new book is almost ready, but he isn't happy with the end and wants me to read it.'

'Why can't he send it to you?' Cassie asked.

'Because he doesn't want anyone other than me to see it, and if he sends it in he's worried I may show it to one of my professional readers. I don't think I'll be back early enough tomorrow to come in to the office, but I'll see you first thing Wednesday.'

'I'll spend the time getting my bearings.'

'No, you won't.' His tone was tart. 'I have two tapes for you to transcribe. They'll keep you busy till my return.'

He should only know! Straight-faced, she took the tapes from him, and the instant he had departed she contacted the secretarial bureau she had seen last week, and told them she was sending two tapes to them by special messenger.

'They'll be ready Thursday morning,' the woman on the end of the line promised.

'I have to have them by tomorrow afternoon,' Cassie stated, and by offering to pay extra was assured they would be with her as requested.

Deciding to use her free time to improve her performance on the word processor, she diligently worked through every page of the manual, and by the following afternoon felt far more at ease with it. At three o'clock the tapes and a hundred pages of beautifully presented letters and reports were delivered to her, and jauntily she placed them on Miles Gilmour's desk, where he would see them as soon as he came in the next morning.

She peeped at her watch. It was four o'clock, and her head and shoulders ached from poring over her computer. She longed to call it a day and go home, but was reluctant to leave until five-thirty in case her boss—she made a face at the word—called her. It was exactly the sort of thing he might do—ostensibly checking to see if she had any problems, but actually checking to see if she had left early!

Sinking back into the chair behind her desk, she reached for the word processor manual and was soon absorbed in it. Oh, boy, what a lot she still had to learn!

'Enjoying yourself reading?'

An acerbic male voice made her drop the manual on to her lap as she lifted her head and met her employer's accusing grey eyes. Curving dark eyebrows were drawn together above his strong nose, and his well-shaped mouth was set in a thin line of disapproval. 'Why aren't you typing the tapes I left you?' he went on, very much the bad-tempered male.

'I've finished them,' she informed him smoothly, exulted by the prospect of cutting him down to size. 'It's all on your desk.'

He had the grace to look discomfited, though he did not apologise. 'I hope you're at least reading one of *our* books,' he said gruffly.

'Yes—it's——' Wildly she struggled to recall a title from Barlow's latest list. 'It's—er—*Chinese Snuff Boxes of the Eighteenth Century*,' she mumbled, recalling the illustrated coffee-table volume she had seen in the reception area, which tallied in size with the manual he had glimpsed in her hands.

'Not your type of book, I'd have thought,' he commented.

'Oh, it's wonderful,' she lied. 'If I could afford it, I'd collect snuff boxes.'

'Why not start with the book? Employees get a twenty per cent discount.'

'It would still come to thirty pounds.'

He gave a slight shrug and went into his office. 'Give me ten minutes to go through my mail, then come in with your notebook.'

Cassie paled. He had told her shorthand was a necessary requisite, but that it was rarely needed as he preferred tapes. Once she had settled in and felt more secure she had planned to tell him she had lied about her ability to do shorthand because she had been anxious to get the job. But if she said as much now he might fire her.

As the door closed behind him she reached for her bag and dashed into the cloakroom. The plan she had devised for such a situation would now be put into operation. Feeling like a spy, she took a tiny dictaphone from her purse, and fixed it to the strap of her bra. Only an inch square, it was sensitive enough to pick up conversation at a distance of several feet. It had cost her a week's salary, but as Catherine Barlow she spent more on a pair of shoes!

Re-buttoning her blouse, she collected her notebook and went in to see Miles Gilmour. He had taken off his jacket and rolled up his shirtsleeves. Standard practice for him when he was working, she guessed. His arms were muscular, the skin covered by a spattering of fine dark hair. His hands, though strong-looking, were very well shaped, with long fingers and spatulate nails. A very masculine man, she thought, and one who would always want to be in control.

'I must commend you,' he said, tapping the bundle of typescript in front of him. 'There isn't one error to be found.'

'Thank you.' She lowered her eyes, not from modesty as he probably assumed, but amusement.

'I remember you saying your shorthand wasn't very fast, so if I go too quickly stop me.'

'I certainly will,' she assured him gravely.

He re-read the letter he was holding, and Cassie thought it a good opportunity to switch on the recorder.

Slipping her hand into the front of her blouse, she searched for the start button. Dash it, there were three, and she couldn't remember if she had to press the first or the third!

'Anything wrong, Cassie?'

She jumped as though shot, and hastily extracted her hand. 'Wr-wrong?'

'You've been fiddling inside your blouse with a look of anguish on your face.'

'I—er—I was looking for a tissue,' she improvised wildly. 'I don't have a pocket in my skirt, so I keep one...' She trailed her voice away, and tried to look embarrassed.

'If you've lost it, get another.'

She hurried out, peeped down the front of her blouse to ascertain which button she had to press, and did so before returning to the office, a tissue ostentatiously in her hand.

Barely waiting for her to be seated, he began dictating.

The sound of the mini recorder was barely audible, but to Cassie's ears it sounded like the revving of a Formula One racing car! Nervously she glanced at the man behind the desk, but from his concentration it was clear he was unaware of it.

He rattled off four letters in quick succession, and her pencil flew over the pages of the notebook in as close an approximation to shorthand as she could recall from the jottings of her mother, who still used it to write messages.

'You seem to be keeping up with me,' he murmured some time later. 'Even my treasured Mrs Darcy found it difficult.'

He rose and stretched his six-foot frame, his cambric shirt tightening across his chest to show the muscles. There wasn't a superfluous ounce on him, Cassie saw, which wasn't surprising considering the punishing pace at which he worked. Did he play equally hard? She abandoned the question as he came to stand beside her, petrified in case he heard the recorder whirring.

'Read me the last sentence, will you?'

Thank heavens he hadn't asked for the whole paragraph! Two lines she could manage with ease.

'Have you devised your own symbols?' he questioned, half bending towards the notebook on her lap. 'Or is it some new-fangled system?'

'I'm not sure how new it is,' Cassie replied, once again refusing to meet his eyes. She hated lying like this, but she had no choice. 'But it's the one I was taught.'

'It's damn good.'

Fluently he resumed dictating, and, heedful of him towering above her, she was hard put not to fumble. Four letters later she glanced at her watch. Another minute and the tape would run out! Her gasp of dismay was audible, and he broke off in mid-sentence.

'Anything wrong?'

'No, but—but—would you excuse me for a moment?'

He nodded, and she hurried to the cloakroom, inserted a new tape in the recorder, and returned to his office.

He resumed working, and Cassie continued writing rubbish in her pad. Another fifteen minutes passed and he showed no sign of stopping. At this rate she'd have to put in *another* tape. Hardly had the thought entered her head when she heard the recorder stop.

'Oh!' She jumped to her feet. 'I'm sorry to interrupt you, but...' Not giving him a chance to reply, she dashed out.

This time when she returned he contemplated her with a frown. 'Do you suffer from a weak bladder, Cassie, or did you drink too much at lunchtime?'

Scarlet-faced, she mumbled inaudibly, and was relieved when he shook his head and resumed dictating. Yet another four letters later she was wondering desperately how much longer he could go on. Another five minutes and she'd have to dash out again!

'That's it,' he said abruptly, tilting back in his chair. 'You can start on the letters first thing in the morning.'

Breathing a sigh of relief, she made for her office. Afraid to call the typing bureau in case he overheard her, she flung on her coat and left the building. She'd have to devise a code that would enable her to call them without giving herself away, she thought as a taxi deposited her at the door of Speedy Type. If she didn't she'd end up a nervous wreck!

An explanation of her predicament to the woman who owned the bureau resulted in an easy solution and, considerably happier, Cassie hailed another taxi to take her to the shop where she had bought her mini recorder.

'If you want one that will run for two hours without stopping it will cost a small fortune,' the young man who had sold her the first one said on learning her problem.

'Do you have one available?'

'Yes.'

'I'll take it.' Cassie had no hesitation in doing so. What she would learn from working for Miles Gilmour would repay this outlay a thousandfold. And there'd be no further cracks about her bladder or drinking too much, either!

The next day followed the pattern of the previous afternoon, except that now Cassie was full of confidence in the knowledge that her bra was sporting the very latest in high-tec surveillance equipment, and that the typing bureau would understand her telephone message when she called them.

'Beats me why Lionel let you go,' Miles Gilmour said when they stopped for a ten-minute tea-break in the afternoon. 'I think you may be a sensational secretary.'

Her sherry-brown eyes widened. 'Only "think"?'

'I don't yet know how you handle people or important telephone calls.'

There was no humour in his voice or on his face as he made this statement, and Cassie saw he was deadly serious. Heavens! What a dictator he'd make!

'I don't think you'll have any complaints about me in those departments either,' she snapped. 'If you——'

She broke off as the telephone rang, and he signalled her to take it, at the same time pressing the switch that enabled him to hear the caller. As a soft, breathless voice sounded in the room Cassie bit back a groan. It was the same girl who had called to speak to him twice this morning, and on both occasions he had instructed her to say he was out.

She did the same now, dismayed when the girl said that the switchboard operator had informed her that Mr Gilmour was definitely in his office.

Cassie thought fast. 'I think she meant he was on his way here, but I'm afraid he must have been side-tracked and is with someone else.' From the corner of her eye she saw a tanned arm gesturing a wave at her, and, interpreting the signal, she said, 'Ah, you're in luck. He's just walked in. I'll put you through to him.'

Ignoring his grin, she handed him the receiver and went out, but not before she heard his deep, incisive voice soften as he said, 'Hello, angel. Sorry I missed your calls this morning. I hope you're still free for dinner tonight?'

It would serve him right if Breathless Voice wasn't, Cassie thought sourly, though he probably knew a dozen girls who'd happily ditch another date to accept one from *him*. Which only went to show how stupid women could be over a six feet two inch male with black hair, slate-grey eyes and oodles of charm. Well, his charm meant nothing to her, for she knew how insincere it was, turned on and off like a tap and used only when it suited him.

Thank goodness he hadn't made a pass at *her*! Even though his stated policy was not to mess with the hired hands, there were always exceptions to even the most stringent rules—particularly where sexual attraction was concerned—and she had half anticipated that a well-proportioned brunette with a 'come hither' walk would have been too strong a bait for him to ignore.

The interruption to their work gave her the chance to munch on a sandwich left over from lunch. The intercom buzzed as she was halfway through it, and dropping the remainder in the wastebasket she went in to him.

'Enjoyed your snack?' he enquired. 'You've a crumb on the side of your mouth.'

Embarrassed, she wiped it away. 'We worked through half our lunch hour and I'm hungry.'

'Complaining, are you?'

'No. Merely stating a fact.'

'Now you've done so, do you mind if we carry on?'

Not waiting for her answer, he rattled off a long letter to an Indian publisher who had produced a copy of a Barlow book without having a contract, and while Cassie's pencil wrote nonsense in her notebook she seethed inwardly at his behaviour. Just wait till she took her rightful place here. Every employer's lunch hour would be sacrosanct, and Mr High and Mighty Gilmour could like it or lump it!

It was five o'clock before he glanced at the thin sliver of gold on his wrist, and announced he had finished for the day.

'Don't take this as the norm,' he warned. 'I'm stopping early so you won't faint from starvation.'

'That's most kind of you.'

'Don't say what you don't mean! You've been sitting there for the past hour wishing you could boil me in oil! And I can't say I blame you. I work too damn hard, and I expect others to do the same. I'm sorry.'

His unexpected apology disarmed her. 'That's all right. Barlow Publishing means everything to you, and——'

'I'm a fool to let it. The company isn't mine, as you know, and Lord knows what will happen if Catherine Barlow decides to run it herself.'

'But *your* position wouldn't be in jeopardy?' Cassie said with studied innocence, hoping his temper had cooled in these last few weeks.

'Maybe not. But the day she comes in I walk out.'

'Even if she offered you a partnership?' Cassie waited on tenterhooks for his reply, deeply chagrined when, instead of answering, he pushed back his chair and rose.

'By the way,' he said from the doorway, 'that book on Chinese snuff boxes you were reading yesterday. When you've finished it I'd like to have your opinion of it. We produce a few minority interest books, and don't make a profit on them, and some of my fellow directors want us to stop doing it completely.'

'Do *you*?'

'Definitely not.'

'I'm glad. Barlow's is so successful that you don't have to print everything with a profit motive in mind. I'm sure Miss Barlow would think the same.'

'You have a direct line to her opinion?' came the dry retort.

'No, but . . .' Cassie cursed her quick tongue. 'I—er—once read something about her. That she believed in education and—and——'

'Heaven spare me from do-gooders,' he cut in. 'And also spare me any further mention of that woman!'

'Of course,' she gulped, her reply drowned by his banging the door shut on his way out.

Unclipping the recorder from her bra-strap, Cassie slipped the tiny cassette into an envelope, then called the typing bureau.

'It's Cassie,' she said, following the procedure she had agreed with the owner. 'The work you asked me to do for you is ready, but you needn't send a messenger for it. I'll drop it in on my way home.'

Only as she replaced the receiver did she see Miles Gilmour on the threshold of her office. Her pulses raced madly, the tempo increasing as he regarded her with narrowed eyes.

'What work?' he demanded.

'I—I——' Her wits seemed to have left her, and she floundered to a stop.

'Don't tell me you have another job apart from this one?' he said into the silence.

Moistening lips that were bone dry, Cassie nodded. 'I—I need the extra money, and do some work for a typing bureau.'

'And you tell *me* off for being a workaholic!' he exploded.

'I do it from necessity,' she defended.

'I'd consider it a necessity for you to learn how to balance your budget! Doing two jobs will inevitably affect your competence.'

'You haven't complained so far,' she retorted.

'True. But if I do, one of the jobs will have to be given up.'

It wasn't until much later that evening, after she had treated herself to a meal in the Greek restaurant, that Cassie's good humour returned sufficiently for her to see things from Miles Gilmour's point of view. He paid her an excellent salary and had a right to expect her wholehearted interest in her job, which might not be possible if she were really doing part-time work for someone else as well. Poor man. He was learning things about his new secretary that were raising his blood pressure. Lord knew how high it would go if he discovered the whole truth about her!

Smiling at the notion, she returned home, and was still smiling at it when she fell asleep later that night.

CHAPTER FOUR

FOR the next few weeks Cassie saw little of Miles Gilmour. He was engrossed in a round of wage negotiations and was rarely in the office, other than to hand her a tape to transcribe and a list of telephone calls to make. Indeed, if this continued she would learn more about typing bureaux and the British telephone service than she would the running of Barlow Publishing!

However, she used her free hours to good effect, buying a software program to teach herself touch-typing, and achieving forty words a minute by the time a pay agreement was reached and Miles returned to the office. Not that she intended slogging away typing all the tapes he handed her, when she could afford to have a bureau do them. But at least she could now do certain urgent letters without making a fool of herself.

Even with the negotiations over, Miles did not slow his pace. Indeed, he gave such a sense of urgency to everything he did that Cassie had to be on her mettle to keep up with him. But at least now he was around again she could continue learning about the publishing business, though when she casually said as much to him, he laughed derisively.

'There's a great deal about publishing that one can never learn. It's called gut feeling, and you either have it or you don't. It's gut feeling that tells you when a badly typed manuscript sent in on lavatory paper is going to be your next bestseller, or when the novel you've been waiting for from your top author is so lousy that you'll do anything rather than publish it, even though your top editor says it's the best thing they've ever read.'

'So what do you do?' Cassie asked.

'Play it like a first-class diplomat. You don't want to lose your top author because sure as hell the next book is going to be great, so you tactfully suggest some alterations and then publish it with the minimum of fanfare.'

'But won't you lose money on it? I mean, if it's bad the public won't buy it.'

'If the author's last book was successful the public will always buy the next one. You only have to worry if the next book after *that* is a lemon.'

'And if it is you let the author go to one of your rivals,' Cassie said triumphantly.

'Not always. That's where gut feeling comes in again. You have to assess whether or not the author is written out and won't ever produce anything worthwhile, or whether to nurse him or her along till they hit the jackpot again.'

Cassie bit her lip, not sure if Miles Gilmour was making his job seem more difficult than it was, or telling her the truth. The trouble was he had a complex personality, and whenever she thought she was beginning to understand him she discovered she didn't.

He was in turn exacting and then easy-going, impatient and unexpectedly considerate, but overlaying all this was his charm. No man could possibly have had more, or known better how to use it to his advantage, either when wheeler-dealing with the numerous aspects of business, or with the many women who flitted in and out of his personal life.

Keeping private telephone calls to the minimum might be preached by him, but he did not practise it, for he received frequent calls from girlfriends. He dealt with them swiftly, but it was clear that he enjoyed being chased, and equally had no intention of being caught!

'If Miss Edmunds calls again,' he informed Cassie one afternoon, when the girl had called for the sixth time and he had refused to speak to her, 'tell her I had to go to Rome unexpectedly, and you don't know when I'll be back.'

'What happens if she sees you in a restaurant?' Cassie asked, shocked that he could be so cruel. 'She knows your favourite ones, and she might go there.'

'Then she'll know I was lying, and will finally accept that I meant it when I told her we were through. And wipe that disapproving scowl off your face. You're my secretary, not my conscience.'

'I don't think you have one,' Cassie said coldly. 'Do you want to get married, Mr Gilmour, or do you enjoy playing the field?'

The question popped out before she could help it, and she lowered her eyes, waiting for him to tell her it was none of her business. Yet surprisingly he leaned back in his chair and considered what she had asked him.

'I'd be a liar if I said I didn't enjoy dating beautiful women,' he admitted. 'Though lately I've found it equally enjoyable staying home with a good book. I mean it,' he added as she glanced up at him. 'So either I need to recharge my batteries or widen my female circle.'

'Or settle down with one woman.'

Wide shoulders lifted in a shrug. 'I've a low threshold of boredom, Cassie, and I've yet to meet the girl who excites me the whole time.'

'How tedious to be excited the *whole* time,' she retorted. 'It's like having caviare with every meal.'

He chuckled, but made no further comment, and she reverted to Miss Edmunds. 'Shall I really tell her you've gone to Rome?'

'Unless you can think of a better excuse.'

'I could tell her she'd be better off without you.'

A black eyebrow rose high. 'Sounds as if you disapprove of me.'

'Why should I? You're a very good employer.'

He smiled at her prevarication. 'But on a more personal level?' he pressed.

'I don't know you on a more personal level, so I can't comment.'

'That's what's known as a cop-out, Cassie.'

'Better than being thrown out, Mr Gilmour! Honesty is not *always* the best policy!'

Further probing was mercifully cut short by a query from the publicity department regarding his appearance on a forthcoming television programme. He was a polished performer, and whenever a pundit from the publishing world was required he was usually the first choice.

There was no question that he was multi-talented, and would have succeeded at anything he put his mind to. Yet even after two months with him she still found him an enigma. Somebody must know the inner man, she mused, and she refused to believe there wasn't one woman who had come close to him, who had touched the inner core of the man.

Yet the frenetic working pace he adhered to belied the possibility of a meaningful love-affair. Meals, including breakfast, were often working ones, and weekends were frequently spent reading manuscripts given him by various editors for his final opinion. In addition, he was much in demand as a speaker and, on one occasion when he regretfully turned down an invitation because of a prior commitment, he told her that before joining Barlow's he had been a university lecturer, and had dreamt of becoming a don.

'What changed your mind?' she asked tentatively, reminding herself that she was his secretary, and not supposed to ask personal questions.

'The narrow confines of academia,' he replied. 'It was too smug.'

'But all that studying for nothing!'

'Hardly for nothing. English was my subject, and it's stood me in good stead here.'

He must have had a disruptive effect on many of his students, Cassie couldn't help thinking, remembering the crush she had had on one of her tutors at college. He'd been a heart-breaker too, like Miles Gilmour, but had finally been captured by a plain little thing with a will of iron. If only it could happen to *this* Lothario! Gemma Charles, his current girlfriend, who ran an exclusive exercise studio, was top of his list since Miss Edmunds had been given the order of the boot, but seemed equally doting and pliable.

'Miss Charles phoned three times,' she informed him when he returned to the office after a lengthy business lunch at the Connaught. 'She said she had expected to see you last night.'

'My dinner with Donald Tremont lasted longer than I thought,' he replied, 'so don't look so disapproving. You're beginning to remind me of my mother!'

It was the first time he had mentioned her, and Cassie had assumed she was dead.

'Why the surprise?' The silver grey eyes missed nothing. 'Did you think I arrived in a puff of smoke?'

'You've never spoken of her before, and I——'

'The topic has never arisen—any more than the topic of *your* family has. At the risk of spoiling the picture you've built up of me, I should tell you that I was a very happy child, with loving parents who are still alive and three doting older sisters.' He sat down behind his desk. 'Now it's your turn—or am I going to get the brush-off?'

'Br-brush-off?' she stammered.

'Whenever I've asked you anything remotely personal I've felt the chill wind of Siberia blowing on me.'

Cassie knew this to be true, but could hardly tell him she was frightened of accidentally giving away her identity.

'I know as little about you now as I did the first day I met you,' he continued. 'I don't even know where you live.'

'Camden Town.'

'Alone or with friends?'

'Alone in a house—a very tiny one,' she hastened to add.

'Do you have a boyfriend?'

She wondered at the sudden interest. 'Yes—in fact he knows you. It's Justin Tyler.'

'Good grief! I wouldn't have thought he was your type.'

He made it sound like an insult to her taste. Clearly Justin's dislike of him was reciprocated.

'How would you know *what* my type is, Mr Gilmour? As you correctly said, you know nothing about me.'

'Perhaps it's time we did something about that.' His head tilted, and a lock of silky black hair fell across his forehead. 'Have dinner with me tonight?'

The invitation was unexpected, and Cassie was momentarily robbed of speech.

'Unless you're busy, of course,' he added.

'I'm not,' she said truthfully, 'but I don't think I should. I work for you, and it's best to——'

Her voice faded as she saw his amusement. It was the same expression he wore when an agent tried to better him while negotiating a new contract for an author—a tussle they invariably lost.

'When you first interviewed me you said you didn't mix business with pleasure,' she reminded him primly. 'And I'm quite happy to leave it that way.'

'Trust a woman to remember things you'd like her to forget! But don't worry, I shan't try to ravish you. My invitation came from a genuine interest to know my perfect secretary a little better. I promise to keep my hands to myself, and have you safely in bed by ten-thirty—alone!'

Unable to withstand his humour, she grinned. 'OK. But first I'd like to go home to change.'

'There won't be time—I want you to work late tonight. I'm leaving for Washington in the morning.'

'That's sudden, isn't it?'

'Yes. Something happened over lunch, and it decided me. I stopped off at a travel agency and booked a ticket on Concorde.'

'Can you tell me why you're going, or is it a secret?'

He occasionally refused to discuss his dealings even with her, particularly if he was trying to poach an author from a rival publisher, and she had often wondered if he had been as reticent with the woman she had replaced, or if he did not yet know her well enough to trust her discretion.

'I'll tell you over dinner,' he promised. 'Meanwhile, get Miss Charles on the telephone for me. I was supposed to be seeing her tonight.'

Cassie's cheeks flamed. The swine! Turning down his current lady to take out another one.

'My dinner with you is a business one,' he said blandly, interpreting her expression. 'It's important for us to have a good relationship.'

Biting back a sharp retort—it wasn't diplomatic to show how contemptuous she was of him—Cassie went into her office to call Gemma Charles. She didn't for a moment believe Miles Gilmour was taking her out to further their business relationship. He had probably asked her knowing it would put Justin's nose out of joint. He might even try to flirt with her for the same reason, and if he did she would walk out on him. But no, it was silly to do that. She was working for him to pick his brains, and no matter how low he sank in her personal estimation, she had to stay with him till she had learned what she wanted to know.

By the time they had finished work for the day it was nearly seven-thirty, for he had wanted to clear his desk before leaving for the States.

'I've booked a table at Harry's Bar for eight,' he informed her, naming one of London's most exclusive clubs. 'Have you been there?'

'No,' she lied. The membership was beyond Justin's pocket, but she had been taken there by her parents' best friends a few weeks ago. Although she had determinedly avoided seeing her own friends while she was engaged in her subterfuge, it had been impossible not to accept an invitation from the couple she had called Aunt and Uncle since she was five.

'I've heard it's very smart,' she murmured, 'and I'd rather go somewhere else as you wouldn't let me go home to change.'

His eyes took in the simple black and white hounds-tooth check shirtwaister, tightly belted in white patent leather to emphasise her small waist and shapely hips. A heavy silver bracelet encircled one wrist, and a matching necklace lay upon her throat, the dramatic design at odds with the simplicity of her dress.

'You'll do.' His words were brief but complimentary. 'But your nose is shiny, so I'll give you ten minutes to do a repair-job!'

She was ready in less, intent on not keeping him waiting in case it spoilt his relaxed mood. This was their first time together away from the office, and she was hoping to learn something of the private man, see the face that lay behind the business mask.

When she entered his office again he was waiting for her. He had changed his cream shirt for a white silk one with a fine blue line running through it, which was a perfect match for his immaculately tailored charcoal-grey suit.

'I like your hair—you should wear it like that more often,' he said as he led her down to the car park beneath the building.

She had always worn it in the chignon of their first meeting, but had freed it tonight, allowing it to fall softly to her shoulders. She was glad of its natural wave, for she could change styles with the minimum of effort. Loose like this it made her appear far younger, though this might also have been due to the added sparkle in her eyes and the slight flush on her cheeks.

Despite disliking him for his attitude to women, she could not help being intrigued that he was taking her to dinner. Whatever his reason for doing so, she would use the evening to further her own ends. After all, this was the only reason why she was working as his secretary.

CHAPTER FIVE

SITTING opposite Miles in the smartly decorated restaurant—he had told her to call him by his first name during the drive—Cassie studied the lengthy menu.

'You're not a vegetarian by any chance?' he enquired. 'It's ridiculous to think I don't even know that about you.'

'No, I'm not. But even if I were there'd be plenty to choose from. I'm spoiled for choice.'

'What do you prefer for a main course? Fish or meat?'

'Fish.'

'I'll join you and order the same. I can recommend the salmon *à l'estragon*.'

'Sounds great,' she replied. 'And I'll have a dozen oysters first.' The instant she spoke Cassie knew she had made a mistake. A secretary being treated to dinner by her boss would never plump for one of the dearest items on the menu. But she had momentarily forgotten her position, and there was no back-tracking.

'You're sure you wouldn't prefer caviare or *foie gras*?' he asked.

Cassie was relieved to hear amusement rather than annoyance in his voice.

'I hope you don't mind about the oysters?' she asked, affecting a naïve tone. 'But I've always wanted to taste them, and have never been out with anyone who could afford it.'

'I was only teasing,' he assured her. 'Have whatever you like. It's a pleasant change to be with someone who isn't completely blasé.'

Having given their order, he gave careful attention to the wine list, consulting her as to her preference, and showing pleasure when she said she liked something dry.

'Most of the women I know go for sweet wine,' he said. 'I try to re-educate their palates, but it's an uphill struggle.'

'Maybe you aren't patient enough!'

'I can be very patient—when it suits me.'

Not sure if there was a double meaning behind his remark, she pretended absorption in buttering a roll.

'I like a girl with a healthy appetite,' he remarked. 'It irritates me to lay out a small fortune on a meal and see it picked at.'

'I promise to clean my plate!'

'I'll hold you to it.'

The oysters when they came were superb, and rendered even more so by the Pouilly-Fuissé with which they were served.

'How do you like it?' Miles asked as she set down a shell.

'It's a taste I could easily acquire!'

'Fancy another half-dozen?'

'I'd rather save room for a sweet.'

'Obviously you don't have to count calories?'

'No—weight has never been a problem.'

'Nothing else either, I imagine. You strike me as an uncomplicated girl.'

'I hope by uncomplicated you don't mean simple?'

'Positively not. You're the most intelligent secretary I've had. It's obvious you're not just doing a job, but enjoying it.' He was silent while the waiter cleared away their plates. 'Would you be interested in transferring to another department? It would mean a promotion.'

'Are you willing to give me up?'

'With reluctance, but yes. I feel the sacrifice would benefit the company.'

'I appreciate the offer,' she said truthfully, 'but I enjoy what I'm doing.' Dextrously she manoeuvred herself out of an awkward situation. With Miles she was covering the whole spectrum of publishing, and the last thing she wanted was to be shunted to a reader's desk, or lost as a junior editor. 'But I wouldn't mind a raise if you're *that* pleased with me,' she added cheekily.

He looked nonplussed, then chuckled. 'You deserve it—for sheer nerve if nothing else!'

The main course arrived, and Cassie attacked it with gusto. 'Delicious,' she praised.

He nodded agreement. 'A lot of people come here to see and be seen. For me it's the food that counts most, and the standard is consistently high.'

'Which reminds me you were going to tell me about today's lunch,' she put in, 'and what decided you to rush off to New York.'

'It's confidential,' he warned, and, at her slight smile, pushed away his plate and rested his hands on the table. They were pale against the navy of his suit, and she noticed how long his fingers were, the nails short and well manicured.

'I had lunch with Ted Black,' he named a top literary agent, 'and heard that the complete works of Selwyn Wilder were up for grabs. His publishers were recently taken over by an industrial conglomerate, and because of a loophole in the assignment clause the new owners didn't get the rights to the back-list.'

'What's an assignment clause?' Cassie questioned.

'It directs where the rights go if your publisher is taken over. Apparently Selwyn doesn't fancy himself as part of an anonymous corporation, and I think we stand an excellent chance of signing him up—back-list and his future work, too. I gather his new book is ready, but hasn't yet been submitted.'

'Getting him would certainly be a coup.' Cassie was genuinely admiring. Selwyn Wilder was not only a best-selling author, but also a greatly respected writer.

'And strengthen my position,' he added, almost as if to himself.

'Does it need strengthening?' she asked, with deliberate innocence.

'Yes.' His voice was hard. 'I own very few shares in the company, though I have an option clause linked to performance. If I can boost profits sufficiently I get another block of shares, and if I do that I'll be in a better position to fight Miss Barlow.'

'How?' she asked, wondering what he would say if he knew he was sitting opposite her.

'Are you merely being polite, or are you genuinely interested?' he countered. 'Wouldn't you rather be entertained with gossip about some of our more famous scribes?'

'I've probably heard most of it in the staff canteen,' she smiled. 'Please go on with what you were saying.'

He hesitated, as if debating how frank to be with her. 'Although Barlow's is a public company,' he said finally, 'Henry Barlow had the largest single shareholding, and he led me to believe that when he retired or died I would have the option of buying them. Unfortunately he died before he could put it in writing, and his shares went to a daughter he didn't even know.'

'But you're still running the company,' Cassie pointed out.

'Yes—but at the whim of a spoiled little rich girl who doesn't appear to know her own mind. If she decides to sell her holding to one of the multinationals I'll be out in the cold.'

'But wouldn't they ask you to stay? Your reputation——'

'I wouldn't want to stay,' he cut in sharply. 'Barlow's is a quality house, and our best-selling authors subsidise lesser-known and experimental ones. Conglomerates aren't interested in literature as such. They're run by accountants who only care about bigger and better profits.'

She hadn't thought of him as an idealist—and, indeed, perhaps that was too strong a word; rather he was a man who had ideals. If he but knew it she was in complete accord with him, but that didn't mean she would give him free rein to do exactly as he wished.

His mention of getting another block of shares if he increased Barlow's profits might make her position weaker. True, she had inherited fifty-eight per cent of the stock, but if Miles persuaded the remaining shareholders to appoint him as their representative on the Board it would be difficult to oust him at any time. The only way of curbing Miles was to increase her shareholding, and thus weaken his position. Fortunately she had deep pockets—or rather her stepfather did, and she could count on his support and generosity.

Cassie was surprised by her determination. Was this the same girl who until a few months ago had little thought in her head but trivial pleasures?

'I wish you luck in New York,' she smiled, breaking the silence. 'Getting Selwyn Wilder would be great for the company.'

'I know.' He returned her smile. 'Now, what gooey delight are you going to choose?'

She was halfway through a delicious raspberry pavlova, with Miles giving her the giggles with his impersonation of one of their prima-donna writers, when a tall, striking redhead with an incredibly slender figure bore down on them.

'So this is your pressing engagement,' she said scathingly.

Without flinching, Miles rose. 'Hello, Gemma. I didn't say "pressing" engagement,' he corrected smoothly, 'I said "previous". You didn't listen properly.'

Stormy blue eyes raked Cassie before focusing on the man. 'You'll be telling me next she's your secretary.'

'Got it in one! Gemma, meet Miss Elliot. You've spoken to her on the telephone often enough.'

The girl looked so astonished that Cassie was hard pressed not to laugh. Only her irritation with Miles robbed the situation of humour, and again she found herself disappointed by his behaviour. Yet disappointed or not she would do her best to save the girl from further hurt.

'Mr Gilmour has to go to New York first thing tomorrow, and tonight was his only chance of briefing me before he left.'

'How nice to be briefed in Harry's Bar,' Gemma retorted. 'Most employers do it in the office.'

Cassie glanced in Miles's direction. Let *him* get out of that one!

'Miss Elliot puts in so much overtime,' Miles said easily, 'that I felt she deserved a treat.'

'The treat being Harry's Bar, or you?' Gemma asked sweetly.

Miles glanced beyond the girl's shoulder to where a thick-set man with grey hair was looking with interest in their direction. 'I don't think you should keep your escort waiting any longer. It isn't polite.'

With a softly muttered but extremely rude word the redhead glided away, and Miles sat down.

'Sorry about that,' he said.

Cassie forced a smile, and in a mellifluous voice said, 'And as the boat sails into the sunset, another relationship bites the dust!'

'Hardly a relationship. Anyway, the boat was on its way out. Gemma was too possessive, and I dislike women who make scenes.'

'Not half as much as I dislike men who cause them,' Cassie replied. 'I'm glad you aren't *my* boyfriend.'

Undisturbed by her comment, he eyed her. 'What would *you* have done in Gemma's position?'

'Walked past you and never bothered with you again.'

'If only she would,' he said with feeling.

Cassie was astounded that such a stunning-looking girl would allow herself to be treated this way, and still come back for more. Nor could she comprehend why Miles was bored with her after only a couple of weeks.

'You're very fickle, aren't you?' she said.

'As I told you before, I've a low threshold of boredom.'

'Perhaps you should turn to academia for your next girlfriend.'

He laughed, his head tilting to one side. A nearby lamp caught the black sheen of his hair, catching the glint of red in it. What a handsome brute he was, and what pleasure it would give her to play him at his own game. To make him fall for her and then drop him as callously as he'd dropped Miss Edmunds and Gemma Charles and all the others who had come before them. But she dared not do anything to disturb her business rapport with this man. She was working for him to pick his brains, and once she had...

Then what? Remembering she had promised Lionel Newman she would offer Miles a partnership if she decided not to sell her shareholding in Barlow's, she frowned, disturbed by the prospect. Yet why should she be? They worked well together now, and could do so in the future provided they kept their relationship on a purely business footing.

'I'm sorry you're angry with me,' he said into the silence. 'But I make no promises to the women I date. They are free and so am I. We see each other for pleasure, and when the pleasure fades...'

'I hope I'm around to see you fall really hard for somebody,' she commented.

'So do I—for it means you'll be around for many years to come!'

How right he was, Cassie thought, and the prospect of disclosing her identity was so sweet that it curved her mouth into a smile.

'Good,' he murmured. 'I can see you're in a better mood.'

'Yes I am,' she concurred. 'And before it's spoiled by the arrival of another one of your ex-lady-loves, I suggest you take me home.'

Arriving at her little house in Camden Town, he insisted on accompanying her to the front door, and waiting while she unlocked it.

'I enjoyed tonight, Cassie,' he said. 'You've a good head on your shoulders.'

As regards compliments, she had had better, and as she undressed she wondered why she should feel piqued by it. It would make life less difficult for her if Miles saw her as a brain rather than a body, so why be annoyed because he did? It wasn't as if she was involved with him on an emotional level.

Or was she? Could it be that she was attracted to him in spite of herself? The thought scared her to death. Miles was an ambitious man, and even if he fell for her he might bitterly resent her being in control of the company he worked for. Yet on the other hand he might like it very much. After all, if he couldn't be the boss himself, marrying her was the next best thing.

'Hell!' Cassie said aloud. 'If I did fall for him I'd have to make sure he fell for *me* before he discovered who I was.'

Upon which thought she fell into bed and dreamed she threw all her Barlow shares into a blazing fire, before she woke up with a shout of rage. No way was she going to forfeit her birthright for any man!

If—and it was a big if—she fell in love with a man who couldn't accept her as she was, and with what she owned, then he wouldn't be man enough for *her*.

CHAPTER SIX

CASSIE was relieved that Miles had gone away and she did not have to face him the next day in the office. By the time he returned, her romantic notions of last night would be but a memory, and she would be back to her normal self.

Although she had plenty of work to do, she found the quietness depressing. With Miles around there was continual bustle: phones rang, editors conferred, agents and authors pestered. Even Justin didn't contact her. He had a few days' overtime due, and was spending it in Somerset with his parents.

A week after Miles had left he telephoned to say he was returning next day and would she buy a magnum of vintage Krug?

'You did what you set out to do, then?' Cassie asked, genuinely excited.

'And more besides. I'll tell you all when I see you.'

'Is there anything you'd like me to do?'

'In what way?'

He sounded so startled that she was sorry she had asked. 'I-I meant at your home,' she stammered. 'Bread and milk and things.'

'My housekeeper does that,' he replied shortly. 'Goodbye.'

The abruptness with which he rang off was so typical of the man, she could almost picture him at his desk in the next room.

She returned her attention to the thick manuscript lying in front of her, which she had picked at random from a pile on his desk. It had been left for him by one of his senior editors, and for fun she had taken it home to read, and jotted down her impressions. She had not looked at the editor's opinion in case it had influenced her, and now, having done so, she saw it differed from hers in several important aspects. Miles might think her presumptuous if she left her report in the folder too, but it was worth taking the chance, for there was always the possibility he might agree with her.

The telephone rang again. This time it was Justin.

'I'm back,' he announced. 'Missed me?'

'You've only been gone three days,' she prevaricated.

Since they had met she had seen him regularly, and the better she knew and liked him, the guiltier she felt at continuing to go out with him. Although he was amusing and intelligent, they held completely opposite opinions on films, music, politics and food. But while she had dated several other men she had met through Pete and Julie, Justin was the one she found most stimulating—even if it was usually for the wrong reasons!

'I missed *you* very much,' he assured her. 'Any chance of seeing you tonight?'

She agreed, and they arranged to meet at La Sorpresa, an Italian restaurant in Heath Street, Hampstead, a short walk from Justin's flat.

In keeping with her new image, Cassie had bought herself a second-hand Japanese car. She was delighted with it, even though it was four years old, and was amazed she didn't miss her Mercedes convertible, with its power steering and four-speaker stereo.

Justin was seated at a table when she arrived, a bottle of wine in front of him.

'You look gorgeous as usual,' he greeted her with a fierce kiss on the cheek. 'It's amazing, but you never have an "off" day.'

'Flattering, but untrue,' she grinned.

'How are you managing with Miles away?' he asked conversationally, as she sat down opposite him.

'Fine, but the office is too quiet without him. Thank goodness he's back tomorrow. He called just before you did to say he's pulled off a big deal.'

'One of many,' Justin observed.

The envy in his voice was apparent, and Cassie was taken aback. 'I imagine you get as much job satisfaction as he does.'

'But not the same rewards!' His eyebrows, slightly darker than his fair hair, drew together in a frown. 'You have the typical layman's assumption that doctors take up medicine because of some divine calling, when it's often no more than a secure way of earning a reasonable living.'

'But you wouldn't do it if you didn't like it,' she argued.

'The vast majority of people do jobs they don't like,' he pointed out.

'But not doctors. I refuse to believe that.'

He laughed. 'You must meet my father. He fits your picture exactly. A dedicated GP who never uses a locum.'

'He sounds wonderful.'

'Both my parents are.' Justin leaned towards her. 'Incidentally, they're keen to meet you.'

'That's not a good idea.'

'Why not? You know how I feel about you.' He caught her hand in his big, warm one. 'I love you, Cassie.'

Cassie had not expected a declaration so soon, and was sorry she would have to hurt him. But it was foolish to pretend emotions she didn't feel, for it would only lead to greater complications.

'I'm fond of you, Justin, but that's all.' She let her hand remain inert in his. 'I'm sorry if I've led you to believe otherwise.'

'You haven't,' he said softly. 'Perhaps I shouldn't have said anything yet, but I wanted you to know you're special to me.'

Though touched by his words, she refused to be swayed by them. 'I think it might be better if we stopped seeing each other.'

He shook his head. 'I won't mention the word love again, and we'll carry on as before. But until you tell me you're in love with someone else I'll go on hoping.'

'You're making it hard for me to say no,' she sighed.

His face glowed with relief, making him look younger than Miles, though she knew they were the same age. Yet it was not merely Miles's looks that marked him as the more mature of the two. In character they were opposites as well, for Justin was easier to read.

'A penny for them.' He broke into her thoughts, and she met his glance guiltily.

'I've just remembered something I should have done before the shops closed,' she excused hastily.

'There's a supermarket open till midnight, near by.'

'I doubt I'll get what I want there. Miles asked me to buy a magnum of Krug.'

'It used to be Mr Gilmour. What changed things?'

Cassie could have kicked herself for her slip of the tongue. There was clear antipathy between the two men, and she had no wish to fan the flames. A lie formed and then dissolved. There was enough deception in her life already. If Justin was jealous it was his problem, not hers.

'In many offices you're on first-name terms these days. But it's still Mr Gilmour on official occasions.'

The waiter served their main course, and they ate in silence for a while.

'I'd be careful of Miles if I were you. He likes variety, as you've probably discovered, and never stays involved with any woman for long.'

'He's not unusual in that respect,' she commented.

'Maybe. But he can be tougher than most.'

'Perhaps he's been soured by a love-affair that went wrong,' Cassie said casually, and was surprised to see Justin colour.

'It was my sister, Sarah,' he admitted. 'I introduced them while we were at Oxford.'

'Sarah Hollister?' she exclaimed, and set down her fork. She had met the woman a few weeks ago when she had come to the office with her husband David, whose merchant bank had floated Barlow Publishing when it had gone public some years ago. She was beautiful and elegant, both in dress and home—a mansion in Belgrave

Square that had been featured in one of the monthly glossies. 'Why didn't you tell me before?' Cassie asked.

'Because it doesn't reflect well on her.'

Agog with curiosity, Cassie none the less curbed it, and was rewarded when Justin decided to be forthcoming.

'I introduced them during Miles's last year at college, and when he stayed on as a lecturer Sarah moved in with him. They were crazy about each other. I'd never have believed Miles could be so besotted. But after a year Sarah wanted more than an academic life could provide, and when she met David she was up and off. Miles took it in his stride, but from that day on he played the field.'

Many things about Miles now fell into place, not least the reason for his attitude towards his girlfriends.

'Does your sister have any regrets now Miles is so successful?' Cassie asked.

'He isn't in David's league yet,' Justin shrugged. 'Personally I think she still cares for him, and I'm pretty sure he hasn't got over *her*. If he had he'd have married by now.'

Cassie thought so too, and was dismayed by the pang it gave her. 'He's a fool to judge all women on the basis of one bad experience!' she exclaimed, then swiftly apologised for her wayward tongue. 'Sorry, Justin. I know it's your sister, but——'

'That's OK. When she's wrong, she's wrong, and I don't defend her.'

'It must have been difficult for Miles when Henry Barlow chose the Hollister bank to act for him,' Cassie went on.

'I guess so. Not that Miles ever gave himself away. Funnily enough, Sarah mentioned it only the other day. Said Miles has never put a foot wrong and that David is a great admirer of his.'

Cassie would have given a great deal to have known exactly what Miles felt about the situation. Pity she hadn't been aware that Sarah was the woman in his past when she and her husband had come to the office. She would have studied them all the more closely!

The appearance of the dessert trolley gave Justin the opportunity to change the subject. It was apparent that he had said more than he intended, and was probably regretting he'd said anything at all.

Lying in bed later that night, Cassie was convinced that Sarah had been responsible for Miles giving up the academic life for a business one. He had obviously wanted to show her he too could have given her all the material things she craved for, had she given him the chance.

Cassie tried to conjure up a picture of him and Sarah as a loving couple, but failed. The petite, curvaceous blonde had been pleasant enough when they had met, but Cassie had considered her both artificial and superficial, and had had the strong impression that Sarah felt Justin was wasting his time on a girl who was merely someone's secretary.

When Cassie arrived for work the next morning there was a distinct buzz in the building, as if everyone was on their toes, anticipating Miles's arrival. For some reason she had butterflies in her stomach, and concluded that the excitement was catching. She must have glanced at her watch fifteen times, calculating whether he had landed, and the time it would take him to get through Customs and drive into town. Of course he might not come straight to the office but go home first, and the uncertainty made her even more edgy.

She was pouring herself a third cup of coffee when he finally appeared, and the three office phones immediately rang in unison, as if pealing in celebration.

He had come direct from the airport and looked exhausted. There were dark circles beneath his eyes and fine lines fanned the corners. He appeared thinner, too, and the charcoal pin-striped suit, though immaculately tailored, hung loose about his powerful frame. It had clearly been a tough week, and if he continued driving himself at this pace he stood a good chance of dropping dead from a heart attack!

'Greeting me with a frown?' he questioned.

'I was thinking,' she answered nonchalantly. 'That always makes me appear worried.'

'On the contrary, it makes you look erudite.' His expression was pugnacious, but spoiled by the corners of his mouth quivering with good humour. 'Get all the heads of departments up here. I'm going to crack open that magnum I hope you bought, and tell everyone the good news.'

Within moments everyone was assembled, glasses were filled, and Miles raised an arm and called for their attention.

'I know you've been wondering what I was up to in the States, and I won't keep you in suspense any longer. First, I've acquired the rights to Selwyn Wilder's works, both past and new.' There was an excited murmur, and he paused until it had died down. 'I also put in an offer for Merlin Publications——' he named a top American paperback house '—and yesterday it was accepted.'

There was a loud cheer, and then questions were flung at him fast and furiously. Everyone clamoured for more details, and it was over an hour before each individual's curiosity was satisfied and the last person finally departed.

'I think we'd better get down to some *real* work now,' he then said, contemplating the piles of papers and letters which Cassie had placed on his desk.

While he studied his mail she cleared away the glasses and tidied his office. Most of the questions she had wanted to ask about the acquisition of Merlin had already been answered, and she was satisfied that Miles had done the right thing. All she needed to know was how much it had cost, and even this was answered when he told her to write and inform Catherine Barlow they had paid six million dollars for it!

'Is there anything else you'd like to say to her?'

'Not a damn thing! As the controlling shareholder she has to be kept informed of all major decisions, but I don't have to make a social thing out of it! All that interests her are our profits.'

Annoyed with him for being so judgemental about someone he had never met—and especially because he was referring to *herself*—Cassie was tempted into commenting.

'I think you're being too hard on her. As you've never met her, how do you know what she's like? Because she's rich doesn't mean she's a moron, or only interested in getting richer. You should take some of your own advice and not judge a book by its cover.'

She stopped abruptly, afraid she had gone too far, and becoming convinced of it as she saw the downward set of his mouth. 'I guess it's not really my business,' she murmured.

'You're right—it isn't!' he snapped. 'But at least have the courage of your convictions. Honesty's rare enough, so don't spoil it with an apology. There is something in what you said, though,' he conceded gruffly, 'so put in a couple of other comments about what we're doing.'

What an impossible man he was! One moment testy, the next conciliatory.

'I don't regard myself as ultra-sensitive,' he went on, 'but I've the distinct impression you aren't the sort of secretary who falls for the boss!'

It was a tactful way of saying he didn't think she liked him, but, while it had been true in the beginning, learning about Sarah had softened her attitude towards him. So much so, she was afraid that if she wasn't careful she might fall for him and end up like one of his lady friends—discarded.

'And leave out love and kisses!' he stated.

'What?' Her sherry-brown eyes widened.

'From the letter. I may have to be polite to the Barlow bitch, but that's as far as it goes.'

So put that in your pipe and smoke it! Cassie said to herself as she went out, more than ever convinced that if she did decide to take an active part in the running of this company she wouldn't see Miles Gilmour for dust.

CHAPTER SEVEN

DESPITE suffering from jet lag, Miles insisted on clearing his desk before leaving the office, and it was after seven before he yawned, stretched, and rose.

'You look ready to drop,' she remarked.

'I am,' he admitted with a weary smile. 'But at least I don't have to drive myself home—I think I'd fall asleep at the wheel.'

Gathering up her notebook, she went into the outer office and locked it away in her desk. All she needed was for another secretary to pick it up and wonder what on earth these hieroglyphics were!

'Do you always lock your notebook away?' Miles's deep voice enquired behind her, and she swung round to see him in the doorway.

'It's a—a habit I got used to when I worked for Mr Newman,' she invented.

'You're quite a paragon.'

He waited for her to slip on her coat and pick up the carton of champagne glasses she had borrowed from the head waiter at La Sorpresa. It was not heavy, merely awkward to carry with her umbrella and purse, and she was irritated when he made no movement to take it from her as they went towards the lift. Perhaps he would offer her a lift home in his car? She knew he lived in Hampstead and it would not be out of his way.

'Damn!' He stopped abruptly. 'I've left my briefcase behind. Don't wait for me.'

Silently Cassie entered the lift, balancing the carton on her hip as she reached the ground floor and stepped out into the rain. A dark green Daimler with a chauffeur at the wheel was drawn up by the front entrance, and she glanced at it enviously, knowing she'd have a problem in finding a taxi in this weather. She did not drive to work because of the difficulty parking her car. The bays beneath Barlow's offices were reserved for senior staff, and the surrounding area was metered. She generally took a taxi both ways, careful to get out round the corner so that no one from the office would see her. On her salary a taxi would be an occasional luxury, not a daily occurrence.

Resolutely she searched for one, but as expected they were all taken. The carton was growing heavier by the minute, and when a sudden gust of wind blew her umbrella inside out and the heavy rain soaked her hair she had never felt more friendless and miserable in her life. She was crazy to be staying in a cramped little house in London when she could be home in New York with her family and friends.

An empty taxi chugged by, disappearing before she could raise her hand to flag it down. This definitely wasn't her night! Swearing under her breath in a most unladylike manner, she stood stock still by the kerb, determined not to miss the next empty one.

The dark green Daimler came abreast of her, a tinted window slid down, and her employer's angular face came into sight.

'You look like a half drowned rat!' he said. 'Missed your bus?'

Cassie hadn't noticed she was standing by a bus stop, but grabbed the ready-made excuse.

'They're all full. I'll have to walk back to the Underground.'

'Don't bother. I'll take you home.'

She was in two minds whether to accept, but a gust of wind sent her scuttling into the back seat. Her wet fingers slipped on the handle as she went to close the door, and Miles leaned across to do it. She was conscious of the weight of his thigh against hers, and saw his profile—the deep lines etching the long, narrow nose, the curving black eyebrows and thick black lashes—

before he settled back in his seat and the chauffeur set the car in motion.

'You live near Primrose Hill, don't you?' Miles said.

'Yes. But please drop me off at La Sorpresa. I have to return the glasses they loaned me.'

He gave the necessary order to his chauffeur, then pressed a button to close the glass partition.

'We should buy a set of champagne glasses for the office,' he suggested. 'See to it, will you?'

She inclined her head, resisting the urge to say 'Yes, sir.' There was no point in antagonising him simply because she was wet and cold and wishing herself in New York. But it was more than that. She was angry with him for not offering her a lift in the first place.

But gradually the warmth of the car dissipated her bad mood, and she began to feel human again. Opening her purse, she took out a packet of tissues and attempted to dry her face and hands.

'Here—use mine—it will do a better job,' her employer said, handing her a large square of white linen with his initials embroidered in one corner.

Seeing it, her eyebrows rose, and he was quick to notice. 'A present from Gemma,' he said wryly.

'Aah!' Cassie dabbed at her face, apologising as she saw she had put a lipstick mark on one corner. 'I'll wash it and return it,' she assured him.

'There's no need.' He took the handkerchief from her and stuffed it back in his pocket. 'My housekeeper's seen lipstick on my handkerchiefs before!'

'Does she live in?' Cassie asked, feeling foolish.

'Yes—Jack's her husband, so it works out well. They have a self-contained flat over the garage.'

'You have a house, then?'

'Why the surprise?'

Her slim shoulders lifted. 'I tend to think of bachelors living in flats.'

'Then you'll be even more surprised to learn that I have three houses—two in the Cotswolds that I'm knocking into one.'

'Will you ever have time to live there?'

'Certainly. When it's finished I'll go there weekends.'

'When you aren't travelling round the world, or entertaining authors and agents at the Savoy or Harry's Bar, or giving lectures! You really should ease up.'

'Yes, boss.'

Cassie hid a smile. If only he knew how true that was!

'When Henry Barlow was alive we shared the workload,' he went on.

'If his daughter decided to work in the firm you could share it with *her*.'

'Still trying to get me to stay on if she takes over?' he asked drily.

'Only because I like my job and don't want to change it.'

'When and if I go I'll take you with me. I realise you'll never find a better employer!'

Cassie laughed. 'There's nothing like being aware of your own virtues!'

'I don't like pretence of any sort, Cassie, and I suspect you're the same.'

She stifled a pang of conscience by reminding herself that only moments ago he had called her a bitch. Well, not her, but Catherine Barlow. But they were one and the same, weren't they? Or was the girl she was pretending to be different from the rich young socialite who had lived such a carefree life in New York?

'Are you an only child?' Miles broke into her thoughts.

'No. I have three older brothers.' This wasn't strictly true, for there was no blood tie with Luther's sons, but she loved them as if there were.

'We're kindred spirits, then,' Miles said, 'although I have sisters. Tell me more about yourself and we'll see if there are any other similarities.'

The car stopped outside the restaurant, and Cassie reached hastily for the carton. Saved by the bell!

'Jack will take it in for you,' her employer said.

'It isn't necessary. I want to get some wine at the off-licence near by, and I'll make my own way home from here. It's stopped raining, thank goodness.'

'Don't be silly. We'll drive you. Wine is heavier than the glasses.'

In her haste to be rid of him she had fallen into a trap of her making, and there was no possibility of extricating herself. To make matters worse, Miles appeared to have got second wind, and followed her into the wine shop, accompanying her round the shelves and advising her what to buy. He knew his wine, and, sensitive to her pocket, chose cheap vintages rather than plonk. Cassie was a bit of a wine buff herself, and with money no object had never considered anything other than the best. But with this man beside her she had no option other than to buy what he suggested. Still, she could always give it to Pete and Julie for one of their cheese and wine parties.

'It's very kind of you to help me,' she gushed as they returned to the car for the short ride to her house where, much to her consternation, he insisted on carrying in the box of drinks for her.

She waited for the comment that was bound to come as he followed her into the living-room. Compared to her parents' duplex in New York this was a cubby-hole, but she knew it was way beyond the salary of a secretary.

'Very nice,' he approved, placing the box of wine on a small table. 'No wonder you asked for a raise!'

He may have meant his remark to be humorous, but it made her feel cheap and money-grubbing. It was ridiculous, of course. Any secretary who worked as hard as he believed *she* did was entitled to every penny he gave her.

'It's owned by a rich relative who's working abroad and lets me live here for a peppercorn rent.' It was the excuse she used with all her new acquaintances, and came glibly to her lips.

'How about the furniture?' he questioned, glancing round.

Cassie hesitated. This was more tricky, for it was obviously all new, her having obtained the agent's permission to put the owner's oak furniture in store and refurbish with the best she could find at Charles Hammond, decorator of Princess Di's home in the country.

'My cousin redid the whole place just before he knew he was being posted to Brazil. Anything else you'd like to know?' she added, deciding attack was better than defence.

'I'm naturally nosy,' Miles excused. 'I hope you don't mind?'

In normal circumstances she wouldn't have done, but she was scared of giving herself away.

'I see you have hidden talents,' he went on, looking at the Regency bookcase standing against one wall.

'Hidden talents?' she echoed.

'The cookery books. I assume it's another of your hobbies—or do they belong to your cousin?'

Cassie could barely restrain a grin. She had recently extended her repertoire to grills and jacket potatoes. Previously, it had been as much as she could do to make toast and scramble eggs. The only reason she hadn't stored the cookery books with the furniture was because they helped fill the shelves.

'*Another* of my hobbies?' she parried.

'Chinese snuff boxes.'

'That's an interest rather than a hobby,' she covered quickly, hoping he hadn't noticed that twice, within a minute, she had not appeared to know what he was talking about! 'They're too expensive for someone like me to collect.'

'So you collect cookery books instead!'

'I enjoy trying new recipes,' she replied non-committally.

'Obviously.' He crossed the room for a closer inspection of the shelves. 'You seem to have all the top chefs. If you're interested I can arrange for you to meet one.' He named a famous chef who often appeared on television. 'You can swap secrets.'

'I don't think he'd be interested in mine!' Her eyes swung to a book on the middle shelf. 'But I'd like to ask him why my *mousseline au roquefort* isn't as light as it should be.' She had noticed the name of the dish printed beneath a picture of the *mousseline* on the front cover, and hoped Miles hadn't noticed it too.

'You're making me feel hungry, though I doubt I've anything as grand as that for dinner.' He glanced at his watch, a wafer-thin Patek Philippe. 'I must be going. I didn't realise how late it was.'

Stifling a sigh of relief, Cassie accompanied him to the door and bade him goodnight. She had the impression he would have stayed for a drink had she offered one. He had certainly milked the subject of cookery books for all it was worth! But she had deliberately played dumb, preferring to keep their relationship as impersonal as possible.

What she had to do was difficult enough without any emotional involvement with Miles. It would only add to the guilt she already felt.

CHAPTER EIGHT

WHEN Cassie arrived for work the next morning Miles was already at his desk, and from the full tape he handed her to transcribe it was plain he had been there some considerable time. As always he looked immaculate, the broad shoulders clad in navy pin-stripes today, the startling white shirt drawing attention to his smoothly shaven tanned skin and the clear grey of his eyes. But the face was still drawn with fatigue, the lines either side of his mouth all too evident.

As she took the tape from him she caught the tangy scent of his aftershave, masculine and sharp, like the man himself.

'Did you manage to get any sleep?' she enquired.

'Not much. But I've only myself to blame. I took a manuscript home with me, and once I started reading it I couldn't stop. It was the one with your comments,' he went on. 'I'm not sure whether to commend you for your initiative or be annoyed at your nerve.'

Silver-grey eyes met hers across the width of the desk, and she could feel their magnetic pull. She pressed her feet firmly on the ground in order not have them swept from under her. He really had far too much charisma for one man!

'While you're making up your mind I'll get on with this tape,' she said into the silence, which she was finding disconcerting.

She moved towards the door, but had barely taken a couple of steps when he called her back.

'Don't ever leave the room while I'm still talking to you.'

His voice was quiet but she was aware of the anger in it, and could have kicked herself. Had she taken her independent stance too far?

'I'm sorry,' she whispered. 'I didn't realise you had any more to say.'

'Well, now you do, so please sit down.'

His voice was still quiet and she perched on the edge of a chair, uncertain what was coming.

'About your report. I agree with most of your comments. It's a first-class read but requires editing and some rewriting. It's very rough in parts—that isn't unusual with a first novel—and with some authors it always applies,' he added drily. 'But I don't agree with your recommendation that we publish it. There I agree with Charlotte.' He referred to the senior fiction editor.

'Why?' Cassie asked. 'If you say you like it...'

'I didn't say I liked it. I said I agreed with your comments. That doesn't mean the same.'

'But it's a sure-fire winner,' she insisted. 'How can you justify not taking it?'

'I don't have to justify it—at least not to you,' he said pointedly. 'But I will, all the same.'

He leaned forward, clasping long, strong-fingered hands together on the desk in front of him. The nails were well tended, and the wrists that extended from his cuffs were strong, with a fine smattering of dark hair. Would they have a gentle touch or be hard and unyielding? Watch it, she warned herself, and concentrated on what he was saying.

'Barlow's have never been frightened to print the controversial, though we've always avoided the sensational. April Davis,' he named the author, 'was a call-girl who had an affair with one of our most respected churchmen. When he refused to pay "maintenance" for a child she claimed was his—but was not proven by a subsequent blood test—she sold her story to a Sunday rag. It ruined his career, his marriage, his entire life. Hardly the most savoury story, is it? And not one that would read well in a publicity hand-out. I hope that answers your question?'

Cassie knew all this, and was irritated that he found it necessary to tell her. In the letter accompanying the manuscript April Davis had included a résumé of her past to spare Barlow's embarrassment in the event that they had forgotten the scandal.

'What you've just told me took place fifteen years ago, when April was nineteen. Since then she's started a successful knitwear business, is a caring mother, and is now trying to become a writer. From some press cuttings she included—reputable papers, I might add, not tabloids—she'll soon be marrying a well-known industrialist. If he's forgiven her for her sins surely Barlow's can do the same?' she ended forcefully.

'By Barlow's you mean me, of course?' Miles said perceptively.

'If the cap fits...'

'It doesn't. I never allow my personal opinions to interfere with the principles I apply to the company. But it's a rule—established by Henry Barlow—that we never publish anything we're ashamed of.'

'Only a narrow-minded bigot would see anything to be ashamed of in April's manuscript!' Cassie flared, her quick temper getting the better of her. 'I'll grant you it's raunchy, but it's also well plotted and amusing and will sell by the million. Think of the erudite, highbrow stuff you can subsidise with the profits you'll make out of it!'

'If you've quite finished,' came the icy comment.

'You can't take criticism, can you?'

'Not from an interfering secretary who has no experience whatever as an editor.' The wide, thin-lipped mouth tightened, indicating that the discussion was at an end. 'Now, if you feel you can continue working for a narrow-minded bigot I suggest you start typing the letters on the tape so they can catch the early afternoon post.'

Fury at the put-down propelled Cassie to the door, and only her determination to hang on to her job stopped her slamming it behind her. She had a feeling any further display of temper on her part would be the straw to break the camel's back—and Miles already had the hump without further provocation!

Keeping her voice low, she contacted the typing bureau. 'The work you gave me to do for you is ready for collection,' she said smoothly, which was her arranged signal that she had a tape that urgently needed transcribing.

'Do you want the work returned in one go?' came the question.

'As much as possible by noon, and the rest to follow.'

As Cassie waited for a messenger to collect the tape she pounded away on the word processor, regretting it wasn't Miles's head. She was typing nonsense words, but at least he would hear the machine going, should he be listening.

At eleven-thirty—the bureau having collected and delivered more than half the work on the tape—Cassie went into Miles's office with a batch of perfectly executed letters. Her temper had abated, and she even managed a weak smile.

'I'm glad to see you're off the boil,' he remarked, raising one eyebrow. 'I purposely left you to simmer in peace in the hope that you'd cool off. You have no respect for authority, have you?'

'I don't blindly follow it, if that's what you mean.'

'There's a right and a wrong way of bucking it.'

'I agree.' Cassie had the grace to be ashamed. 'I came on too strongly this morning and I'm sorry. My only excuse is that I had the impression you didn't want me to be a "yes" woman, and I acted accordingly.'

The wide mouth quirked at the corners. 'There's a difference between stating your opinions and bludgeoning me over the head if I don't agree with you!'

Colour rushed into her creamy skin, and she was aware of Miles eyeing her with more than usual interest. 'You're quite right, but I can't do more than grovel and say it won't happen again.'

Unexpectedly he laughed. 'Don't make promises you won't be able to keep! You can no more prevent yourself from telling me if you disagree with me than I can from losing my temper if I think you've overstepped the mark. But we can at least agree not to take umbrage at one another.'

'Done!'

Cassie was delighted the row between them was over, and not only because she could remain here, but because... She didn't want to complete the sentence, but her innate honesty made her do so, forcing her to acknowledge that she enjoyed working for Miles despite the subterfuges she was forced to adopt, and that she would be most unhappy if, on learning her identity, he refused to stay with the company. She was busy analysing this feeling when he spoke again.

'I'd like you to do something for me, Cassie. Seamus O'Mara has finished his new book but won't trust it to the post or courier services. He's flying in to Heathrow from Cork at three-thirty this afternoon en route for New York, and wants to hand me the book personally. I've explained to him I've a board meeting I can't get out of, and that you'll collect it on my behalf. I gather you spoke to him while I was away, and he took quite a shine to you.'

'I'm surprised he remembered,' she answered with a smile. 'He sounded tipsy.'

'Not unusual for Seamus,' Miles responded. 'If he cuts himself he bleeds Black Label! Fortunately it doesn't affect his writing.'

'I'm looking forward to meeting him.'

'Here's his flight number. Check to make sure it's on time.' Miles handed her a slip of paper. 'Take a cab and charge it, of course.'

'There's no need. I'll use my car.'

'Suit yourself,' he said indifferently. 'But fill up the tank, and we'll pay for the petrol.'

Intent on being early, Cassie decided to forsake lunch and have a snack at the airport. Although the traffic was heavy she made good time until she reached the Chiswick flyover, but as she halted at the red light leading to the entry ramp the Toyota gave a choking sound, shuddered, and went dead.

Frantically she turned the ignition off and on, but to no avail. The light turned green and the Ford behind her hooted irritably. Cassie leaned out of the window.

'Sorry,' she called. 'There's something wrong with my car.'

The driver of the Ford opened his door and came over to her. Short and overweight, he wasn't in the best of tempers, though he softened noticeably as Cassie gave him her warmest smile.

'Open the bonnet,' he instructed, 'and I'll take a look. From the smell of burning rubber I think your fan belt's gone.'

He was proved right, and, after pushing the car into the side of the road, with Cassie steering, he offered to call the AA on his car-phone.

'They should be with you in half an hour,' he called out to her after doing so. 'Good luck.'

She glanced at her watch. It was only one-fifteen, and even if she had to wait an hour she would still make it on time.

Settling behind the wheel, she switched on the radio and tried to relax. But after an hour had passed she grew increasingly anxious. She knew when Seamus O'Mara was arriving at Heathrow, but had no idea when his connecting flight left for New York. She was about to go in search of a telephone booth and have him paged at the airport to explain the delay when she caught sight of a yellow breakdown van in her rear-view mirror. Rescue was at hand!

Unfortunately the patrolman didn't have a suitable fan belt, and had to go to a nearby garage to obtain one. But eventually he returned with it, and ten minutes later Cassie was on her way again. She was later than she had intended, but with a bit of luck Seamus O'Mara would have realised something had happened and be waiting in the Arrival Hall as arranged.

Luckily she found a parking space easily, and raced into Terminal One. It was crowded with holidaymakers, and she glanced hopefully in the direction of the Information Desk. There were several men at the counter, but none resembled the pictures she had seen of the author. She refused to panic. He might have wandered off to the bookstall or gone for a drink. She approached the desk and asked one of the girls to page him.

'Are you Cassie Elliot?' a blonde young woman asked at once.

'Yes. Is there a message for me?'

'Not a very nice one, I'm afraid, but here goes.' Eyes were lowered to the slip of paper in front of her.

Stuff Barlow's. I'll find myself a *reliable* publisher. And to hell with excuses. I won't change my mind.

The blonde head lifted. 'He made me write it, so I wouldn't forget. He was in a dreadful rage.'

Cassie's heart thumped. 'Where can I find him?'

'You can't.' She glanced at the computer terminal in front of her. 'His jet's just this minute taking off. But I think he contacted your office before he left, because he asked me for some change.'

With a murmur of thanks Cassie headed back to the car park, her spirits drooping as she anticipated facing Miles. Still, the delay hadn't been her fault. She had set out in ample time, and it was bad luck her car had broken down.

But all the reassurance she tried giving herself faded as she entered his office and saw his grim face. His lips were set in a thin line and the silver-grey eyes were hard as steel.

'What the hell happened?' he bit out. 'I was dragged from a board meeting to take Seamus's call, and by the time he'd finished wiping the floor with me... Why didn't you call the airport if you were delayed? You know what his temper's like.'

'I did think of phoning,' she apologised, 'but I was afraid to leave my car. It died on me in Chiswick and I had to wait for the AA.'

Miles raised his eyes heavenwards. 'Don't tell me you ran out of petrol?'

'Of course not. The fan belt broke.'

'Why in God's name didn't you lock the bloody car and take a cab?' he demanded scathingly.

'Have you ever tried getting a cab on the Chiswick flyover?' she defended herself, scared of telling him it hadn't entered her head to do so.

'Then, when the AA turned up, why didn't you get *them* to put in a call to Seamus? If you'd explained the urgency of it I'm sure they'd have obliged.'

'I thought I'd get there before he left.'

'Well, you thought wrong!' Miles roared, slamming his hand so hard on the desk that a stack of papers fell to the ground. 'Do you know how much your stupidity has cost us in future royalties? Millions! Millions!'

Cassie was as angry with herself as Miles was with her. Everything he had said was true. She should have had the sense to leave the car and go in search of a cab. And if she hadn't found one the situation had warranted her stopping a passing motorist. Anything, in fact, rather than run the risk of upsetting their most valuable author.

'I'm terribly sorry, Miles. Perhaps if I called him and explained what had——'

'No!' Miles bellowed. 'You've done enough damage already without making it worse.'

'How can I make it worse? If I spoke to him——'

'I said no! Don't you understand English?'

'But I have to do something. We can't just stand by and——'

'Not *we*,' he cut across her. 'Me. Whatever has to be done I'll do myself.'

'You could always print April Davis's book,' Cassie suggested with sudden inspiration. 'It's not only a bestseller in my opinion, it also has the makings of a TV series.'

'Are you serious?' Miles shouted. 'If you think that rubbish could ever compensate for losing a writer like Seamus you must be bloody mad! And what's more I don't want you telling me how to run my business.'

'It isn't yours,' Cassie retorted automatically, then wished the ground would open up and swallow her as she saw the unadulterated fury on Miles's face. His lips narrowed, his eyes half closed, and his skin took on a grey tinge that not even his tan could disguise.

'Thank you for reminding me of that.' His tone was mild, and more frightening because of it. 'However, though Catherine Barlow is the majority shareholder, the contract I signed with her father when I joined the company gives me the right to hire and fire personnel. And it now gives me great pleasure to fire *you*.'

Aghast, Cassie stared at him. His implacable expression and very quietness indicated that this was one order he had no intention of rescinding. For an instant she almost confessed her identity; indeed, when she thought about it afterwards she wasn't sure what had kept her silent.

'Won't you give me another chance?' she pleaded huskily.

Before he could reply the telephone rang, and automatically she leaned forward to answer it. It was a message relayed from the captain of the aircraft taking Seamus O'Mara to New York, saying he had asked the author to take a call from Mr Gilmour, but the author had refused, reiterating even more dogmatically that he never wished to be contacted again by anyone from Barlow Publishing.

In trembling tones Cassie recounted the message to Miles.

'That's it, then,' he said heavily. 'Seamus always was an obstinate bastard, and it will make matters worse if I keep trying to make him change his mind. I just hope he comes to his senses before he gives his new book to another publisher. Though if it gets out that he's quarrelled with us there'll be a stampede to his door.' His eyes met hers, still silver-grey with anger, still hard. 'Please go, Cassie. I'll arrange for you to be paid for three months, but don't expect me to give you a reference.'

'So it's goodbye, then?'

Miles bent his head to some documents on his desk. 'Goodbye,' he said tonelessly.

Returning to her office, Cassie sank into a chair and covered her face with her hands. What a hash she had made of things. And what a mean-spirited man Seamus O'Mara was to use her late arrival as a reason for leaving a company that had served him well ever since he had started writing.

But Miles was no better, using this same incident to be rid of her. Well, he'd had more of a reason perhaps, she conceded wryly, recollecting his fury at her suggestion that by accepting April Davis as their author it might go some way to compensating Barlow for losing Seamus. She saw now that it had been a stupid thing to say. Like waving a red rag to a frustrated bull.

Glancing at the closed door, she knew there were only two courses left open to her. Tell him who she was—and in his present state of mind he'd walk out the moment she did—or try to persuade the Irishman back to the fold. She sighed, accepting that there was no contest, and that she dared not run the risk of Miles leaving the company until she had made up her mind what she wanted to do with it.

Who are you fooling? she asked herself. Wanting him to remain with Barlow Publishing has nothing to do with the company. It's more than that, and you know it. But how much more, and precisely what she knew in her heart, she wasn't prepared to admit.

So that left only the second course open to her. Seamus. If she spoke to him personally and explained what had happened he might reconsider. But he was in New York, and she was in London. So what? That might be an obstacle for Cassie Elliot, Miles's erstwhile secretary, but it was nothing at all to Catherine Barlow. She would leave on Concorde tomorrow morning, see the author, and fly back the same day. If her mission was successful she'd go straight to Miles's house with the new manuscript, and witness the triumph of having him eat humble pie!

But equally important as redeeming herself was the knowledge that he would have to offer her back her job. Or would he?

CHAPTER NINE

BECAUSE it was late Cassie rang British Airways from the office, using the public call box opposite the reception desk for fear of being overheard by Miles. There was no difficulty booking her flights, and she arranged to collect her ticket at the airport.

As soon as she arrived home she rang her mother, briefly recounted what had happened that day, and asked her to find out where Seamus O'Mara was staying. There was no point in trying to fix an appointment with him, for in his present mood he would refuse to see her. Her only hope was to call on him uninvited.

'I'll meet you at the airport,' her mother said. 'We've all missed you so much, darling. It will be wonderful having you home, even if only for a few hours.'

No sooner had Cassie replaced the receiver than Justin called to ask her out to dinner tomorrow night.

'Sorry, I'm busy,' she explained, unwilling to tell him why.

'I hope you're free Friday. Sarah and David are giving a party, and we've been invited.'

Fleetingly Cassie wondered if Miles would be there too, but knew better than to ask Justin.

'What should I wear?' she said instead.

'Something glamorous. It's a black tie affair. I'll call for you at eight. Until then don't do anything I wouldn't do!'

What a pity she couldn't fall for Justin, Cassie thought as she perched on a stool in the kitchen and ate a Marks and Spencer seafood pasta. But emotions couldn't be forced, and no way could she contemplate an intimate relationship with him.

Dinner over, she packed a holdall ready for her early morning departure, then booked a cab to take her to the airport. She wasn't going to rely on her Toyota!

Although she had flown Concorde many times before, she had never become blasé about it. True, the seats weren't as comfortable as First Class on other planes, but this was compensated for by the exceptional food and service, as well as the wonder of arriving in New York at nine thirty-five a.m., fifty minutes ahead of her departure from London!

Her mother was waiting for her at Kennedy airport, but refused to divulge the whereabouts of Seamus O'Mara until she had been told the whole story of her daughter's row with Miles Gilmour.

'He sounds a dreadful man,' Margaret Elliot observed, leaning back against the cream leather of her silver-blue Rolls-Royce. 'How can you bear to go on working for him? It's not as if you have to, darling.'

'But I do. It's the best means I have of learning the publishing business.'

'You don't still have this crazy idea of running Barlow's yourself?' The mauve-shadowed eyes darkened with disappointment. 'Luther and I were hoping you'd sell your shares and come home. I'm sure you can do something equally interesting here.'

Cassie grinned. 'I love living in London, Mom, and even if I came back here I'd want my own place.' She caught hold of her mother's hand and squeezed it fondly. 'Your fledgeling has flown the nest forever; not because she wasn't happy in it, but because it was time to spread her wings.'

'Are you sure it isn't because of *that* man?' her mother questioned. 'Is there more between you than you've told us?'

Cassie's heart missed a beat. 'What a strange question.'

'Does that mean yes or no?'

'He's taken me to dinner once,' she prevaricated, 'but it wasn't a great success.'

'Why not?'

'One of his current girlfriends turned up in the same restaurant, and was furious to see him there with me. Since then I thought it best to keep our relationship strictly impersonal.'

'Truly?'

'If there was anything between us he wouldn't have been so quick to fire me.'

'The nerve of him! You should have told him who you were, and given *him* the boot.'

'I was tempted,' Cassie confessed. 'But then common sense prevailed.'

'Was that the only reason?' Margaret Elliot eyed her daughter suspiciously. 'I believe he's extremely handsome.'

'Very.'

'Then why is he still single?'

'Because he enjoys his freedom,' Cassie replied, aware of a strange pang as she spoke. 'Now will you forget Miles and tell me where Seamus O'Mara is staying?'

'At the Waldorf Astoria,' her mother informed her resignedly.

'I want to go there straight away. If he won't see me I'll camp in the lobby.'

'Don't be silly, honey, of course he'll see you.'

Cassie was nowhere near as sanguine, and, leaving her mother to return home, she entered the Waldorf. She headed for the florist shop, where she bought the most magnificent basket of flowers they had, then took it to the porter's desk and asked for it to be delivered to Mr O'Mara.

The ploy worked, and a few moments later she was surreptitiously following a page boy down a corridor on the tenth floor. As he stopped outside a corner suite, so did she.

'Oh, my flowers have arrived for Mr O'Mara,' she smiled. 'I might as well take them in to him myself.' Pressing a dollar into the young man's hand, she took the basket from him with so much assurance that he didn't think to object, and as he turned away she rapped on the door.

It was opened almost at once by a pretty, dark-haired girl of about twenty, and Cassie quickly introduced herself as Miles Gilmour's secretary, and asked to see Mr O'Mara.

'I'm his daughter Caitlin,' the girl said, glancing nervously over her shoulder, 'and I don't think my father will see anyone from Barlow's. He's in a rare temper with them.'

'I'm aware of that,' Cassie said with feeling. 'It's why I've flown over—so I can talk to him personally. It's terribly important to me,' she persisted, looking as woebegone as possible.

'What's going on out there?' a soft voice with a lilting Irish brogue called, and Seamus O'Mara strolled out of the sitting-room.

Medium in height, with a thatch of dark red hair streaked with grey and a matching well-trimmed beard, he looked older than the fifty-three Cassie knew him to be. A lined face showed signs of the good life, and glinting blue eyes an appreciation of a good-looking young woman.

Taking heart from this, Cassie gave him a wide smile, glad she was wearing one of her Chanel suits, for its cropped jacket and short, swinging skirt showed her figure to advantage.

'I'm Mr Gilmour's secretary,' she announced, and, not giving him a chance to interrupt her, rushed into an explanation and apology over the mix-up of the day before.

'With hindsight I realise I should have phoned you at the airport when I called the AA,' she concluded, 'but I'd allowed myself three hours to get there, and I never thought I wouldn't make it. Mr Gilmour was absolutely furious with me, and fired me on the spot.'

Seamus O'Mara's jaw dropped. 'Miles fired you?'

'I was afraid he was going to kill me,' she said, lowering her eyes as if to hide her tears. 'He went up in blue smoke.'

'But if he fired you why are you here?'

'To see you. I love working for Barlow's. It's one of the best publishing firms in the world, and Mr Gilmour's a brilliant man. I'd hate to work for someone else. That's why I had to see you and beg you to help me.'

'You spent your own money coming here?'

'Yes. And it will be worth every penny if it brings me back my job.'

'You mean if I don't go to another publisher?'

'Yes.'

The author stroked his beard. 'So you think Miles is brilliant, do you?'

'Every author who works with him says he's a fantastic critic,' Cassie extolled. 'And constructive, too.'

'He was the opposite with *you*, but I guess I'm to blame for that. I wasn't particularly constructive with you myself, was I?' Seamus O'Mara's eyes twinkled. 'Now we're finally face to face I shall give you my new book to take back to England with you.'

Cassie was too choked to speak, and the tears she had pretended earlier flowed genuinely. Studying her, the Irishman sighed and wished he were fifteen years younger, but contented himself with offering her coffee.

An hour later, clutching the manuscript, Cassie waltzed in to her parents' penthouse, delighted to find her stepfather there with her mother.

'If Mahomet won't go to the mountain...' he joked, hugging her close.

'I was going to pop into the office to see you,' she averred.

'I see you got what you came for,' he commented, staring at the package in her hand.

'Yes. And I can't wait to see Miles's face when I shove it under his nose.'

'Pity you can't hit him on the head with it,' her mother sniffed.

Cassie laughed, and her stepfather came into the conversation, questioning her about Miles, and how she saw the future.

'I still haven't decided what I want to do,' she hedged. 'It depends.'

'On Mr Gilmour?' her mother ventured with a raised eyebrow.

'Yes, but not for the reasons you think! The more I learn about publishing, the more I realise Barlow's needs him, and right now he's adamant that he'll walk out if Catherine Barlow takes over.'

'I'm sure you can charm him into changing his mind.'

Cassie mused on this as Concorde winged her back to England. Using her womanly wiles on Miles might rebound on her, for *he* had charm too, and she could end up being badly hurt. The knowledge made her face the fact that she was definitely attracted to him. Heavens, what woman wouldn't be? But was it more than attraction? Was she falling in love with him? Was this why it was so important for her to redeem herself in his eyes?

'Of course I don't love him,' she muttered under her breath. If she felt anything for him it was physical attraction, and, come to think of it, it was damned odd that the feeling wasn't reciprocated. Until now men had fallen over themselves chasing her, yet Miles appeared to regard her as a piece of office equipment—reliable if regularly serviced with a few kind words!

Unwilling to continue thinking of him, she picked up the Seamus O'Mara manuscript, and was soon held in thrall by the magic he wove with words. What a tragedy if he had given it to another publisher! It was his best novel to date, and a certain contender for a glittering prize. Undaunted by her previous clash with Miles, she jotted her comments down on a piece of paper, and placed it prominently at the front of the folder.

She refused to contemplate the possibility that he might not reinstate her. His nose would be out of joint because she had succeeded in bringing Seamus back into the Barlow fold where he had failed, but he was too fair-minded to let it rankle for long. Wasn't he?

CHAPTER TEN

IT WAS ten-twenty in the evening when the plane touched down at Heathrow, and with no luggage to wait for Cassie was soon speeding along the motorway.

Arriving home, she called Miles's number to ascertain he was there, and when he answered replaced the receiver and hurried out to her car, Seamus's manuscript in her hand.

The outside of Miles's house held no surprise. Curious to see where he lived, and knowing it was nearby, she had driven past it some while ago. The four-storeyed dwelling was the end one in an eighteen-sixties Victorian crescent situated near Hampstead Heath, and the red brick and white-painted wood exterior was as discreet as the tall, narrow windows and shiny black railings surrounding the immaculately kept front garden.

She parked behind a white Mercedes coupé. It was the same model as the one she drove in New York, only the colour and the personalised number plate was different. SH 1.

Sarah Hollister. Cassie's heart thumped painfully in her chest. Could it really be her? There must be loads of people with the same initials, and it was foolish to jump to conclusions. Yet from what Justin had said to her the feelings between his sister and Miles had not died, and if David Hollister was out of town...

Dismayed by the anger she felt, Cassie reminded herself that what Miles did in his private life was no concern of hers. If he was entertaining a married woman in his home after midnight it was his own affair. Nor was she going to let it deflect her from her purpose. She had come here to deliver Seamus's script, and deliver it she would.

Bracing herself, she opened the wrought iron garden gate, stalked up the stone-paved path, and mounted the short flight of steps to a panelled front door with heavy brass trimmings.

Only as she rang the shiny brass bell and heard it reverberate in the stillness of the night was she aware that other than the lantern illuminating the door, the house was in darkness. An image of Miles in bed, and with whom, swamped her mind to the exclusion of all else, and she was on the verge of running away when the glow of a light through the stained glass panel warned her someone was coming.

Drawing a deep breath, she faced the door as it opened to reveal Miles's rangy, broad-shouldered figure. Incredulously he regarded her.

'What the hell are you doing here at this hour?'

Not the most welcoming reception, Cassie thought, but hardly to be wondered at, given the circumstances! A short, navy silk dressing-gown disclosed long muscular legs and bare feet, a sure sign that he had got out of bed to answer the bell. His hair was tousled, his face flushed, as though he had been awakened from a deep sleep.

Who am I kidding? she thought wryly, and remembering the Mercedes parked outside had an instant vision of Sarah's dainty, petite body melded with a muscular, wide-shouldered one. What a rotten pair they were, playing it so cool when David Hollister was with them, yet using his absence to resume their affair!

'What the hell do you want?' Miles bit out again.

'To give you something—preferably inside,' she stated crisply. 'It's chilly out here.'

Muttering beneath his breath, he stood aside to let her in.

The exterior of the house might be conventional mid-Victorian, but the interior was definitely eclectic, with a preponderance to the modern. The dado and mouldings in the large, octagonal hall were painted white, but the walls were glossy dark brown, a handsome foil for the many modern paintings cleverly lit by well-placed down-lighting, and among which she recognised a Rothko, a Hockney, and a Lucian Freud. The thick pile carpet was in a deep shade of red, and he led her into a study decorated in the same warm colour, with armchairs and settee in mixtures of cream and dark chocolate, standing on a geometric-patterned carpet which she recognised as a David Hicks.

'You said you had something for me?' Miles queried, making no move to sit, and not suggesting that she did.

Hardly surprising, she thought bitterly, when Sarah was waiting in his bed. With a loud thump she placed the paper-wrapped parcel she was carrying on the brass-trimmed mahogany desk that stood in front of the window.

In two strides Miles was there, the angry frown which brought his thick black eyebrows together in one line flying upwards in astonishment as he tore aside the paper and saw the manuscript.

'Where did you get this?' he barked.

'Seamus O'Mara handed it to me a few hours ago.'

'*Handed* it to you?' Long fingers raked back an errant lock of dark hair. 'I don't understand. Seamus is in New York, so how the hell did you see him?'

'I flew there this morning and gave him *my* version of why I hadn't met him at Heathrow. After which we had coffee together, and he gave me the book.' It was hard for Cassie to restrain her triumph as she saw the utter amazement on the hard-planed face in front of her.

'You flew there? Had coffee with him?' Miles's surprise couldn't have been greater had she announced she had had coffee with a Venusian!

'It wasn't difficult,' she said gently, as if she were explaining to a child. 'I called a friend in New York last night, and asked him to find out where Seamus O'Mara was staying. Then I booked a ticket on Concorde and went there.'

'Concorde?' It was a strangled sound, and Miles went on staring at her with the glazed look of a man who didn't believe what he was hearing.

Cassie relished his confusion. After all, it wasn't every day that a secretary you had fired took Concorde to the States to meet your most celebrated author. Ex-author, she amended, and determined to make Miles writhe for the way he had behaved to her.

'Seamus was so impressed by my initiative,' she said without inflexion, 'that he decided not to go to another publisher.'

'I can't believe it.' Miles shook his head. 'I don't know what to say.'

'Thank you isn't a bad start.'

'It isn't adequate, either.' The mobile mouth lifted at one corner. 'You're a miracle-worker!'

'No. Merely a secretary intent on getting back her job.'

He had the grace to show embarrassment. 'That goes without saying. Though to be honest I'm surprised you're willing to come back to me.'

Carefully she delivered her *coup de grâce*. 'It isn't you, Mr Gilmour, so much as the job. I find it extremely interesting.'

There was a short silence. 'Actually, I think you deserve a promotion. You aren't being utilised to your full ability. How would you like to become an editor? You seem to have good critical judgement and——'

'I'd prefer to stay with you for the moment,' she intervened. 'When I accept promotion I want to feel confident of doing a good job, and right now I don't feel I know enough about publishing.'

One corner of his mouth tilted. 'Strange. I had the impression you thought you were ready to step into *my* shoes!'

'If that's a firm offer I might consider it!'

He chuckled, then grew serious. 'Not many people would pass up the chance of advancement and a higher salary, even if they knew they weren't ready for it. They'd muddle along.'

'Money's the least of my worries,' she said thought-lessly, then quickly corrected herself. 'I—I mean I live within my salary, and I'm quite happy with it.'

'You're unique among our employees, then!' he commented drily, and inclined his head to a chair.

'I have free accommodation,' she reminded him as she sat down. 'If I had a mortgage or rent to pay it might be different.'

'Yes, you're a fortunate young lady.' He walked across to the drinks tray standing on a mahogany side-table. 'Care for a drink? I'm having a brandy, myself.'

'A fruit juice, if you have one,' she said, and he nodded and went out, careful to close the door behind him.

Gone upstairs to put Sarah in the picture, Cassie thought cynically, and resisted the urge to tiptoe across the room and open the door to see if she was right.

It was several minutes before he returned, bearing two cups of fragrant coffee on a tray. 'Decaffeinated,' he said cheerily, 'so it won't stop you sleeping. But you said you were cold when you were outside, and fruit juice from the refrigerator didn't seem such a good idea.'

Touched, she took the coffee from him. 'This is wonderful.'

But he had also gone to his bedroom, as evidenced by the black silk pyjama bottoms he was wearing, and the black mules on his feet. Too aware of him, she watched him take a chair opposite her.

'If you do change your mind about a promotion,' he said, 'let me know. You have a good brain and the intelligence to utilise it. Why didn't you go on to university?'

Cassie hesitated, uncertain of the English education system. 'I—I didn't enjoy studying, and opted for the university of life.'

'I hardly consider working for Lionel Newman a particularly broadening experience.'

'I went around the world before that,' she answered, and seeing his puzzlement, knew she had said the wrong thing, but didn't know what.

'You mentioned you'd worked your way around America,' he commented.

'That was just one of my stops,' she fabricated hastily, recollecting she had told him this when he had expressed surprise at her intimate knowledge of the States.

'Which country appealed to you most? No, don't answer that.' He held up a restraining hand. 'That's a subject for an earlier hour.' He drank his coffee. 'Why don't I take you out for dinner on Saturday if you're free? It's part reward again, but I'd also like to make amends for the last time I took you out.'

'Saturday's fine,' she answered, glad that he was unaware of her racing pulse.

'Good. We'll fix the time and place at the office.' He glanced at his watch. 'You must be exhausted. I've done the day-return trip on Concorde, and it's a strain.'

He rose, tightening the belt of his dressing-gown. Navy self-patterned silk, piped in red, the thin material clung to his body as he moved, and the muscles were clearly visible, as was the dark, wiry hair on his chest. She witnessed—and not for the first time—that there was not an ounce of superfluous flesh on him, yet he was not thin. Simply ideal, she thought wearily, and had a feeling that from now on it would be difficult not to compare him with every other man she met.

'I *am* tired,' she admitted, and, stifling a yawn, followed him to the front door.

'I forgot to ask how you paid for the ticket,' Miles said, 'but let me have the receipt tomorrow, and I'll give you a cheque.'

'There's no hurry,' she assured him. 'I charged it to my credit card.'

'They don't allow unlimited credit,' he warned, 'and the return fare on Concorde is pretty hefty.'

'Gold card customers don't have limits.'

His chuckle of amusement made her realise her error. Heavens! She must be exhausted to make so many stupid mistakes. The sooner she said goodnight and left, the better.

'How right you are,' she improvised hastily. 'But at least I made the journey in one day and saved you seven hundred and fifty pounds. If I'd stayed overnight you'd have had to pay the full fare.'

'It might have been worth it not to have been woken up!'

His comment made Cassie remember the woman waiting for him upstairs, and she swallowed a sharp retort. 'Knowing you have Seamus O'Mara back, you'll sleep even more soundly I'm sure,' she managed to say.

'Which reminds me. Take tomorrow off. You'll need a rest after today.'

Safely in the confines of her car, she heaved a sigh of relief. It had definitely been an extremely long day. She was also weary of pretence, and longed to be herself with Miles. Playing a part was a constant strain, even if it was frequently amusing.

Her sojourn in London had given her a new slant on life. She had always known how privileged she was, but the experience of having to fend for herself had been an education she could never have learned from books or hearsay. Not that she was suffering hardship in her newly furnished house in one of the most select areas of London! But none the less it was a far cry from the opulence of her parents' Park Avenue penthouse and country estate in Kentucky. Yet in spite of having to shop and clean for herself, drive an old, inexpensive car, and wear clothes she would never have contemplated before, she had never been happier. She had an interesting job, new and interesting friends who were quite dissimilar from the super-rich circle she had previously moved in, and she had met Miles.

Miles. He was the all-important difference. Everything else she had listed was totally unimportant compared with him. So unimportant that she was scared out of her wits.

Whatever happened in the future, her perceptions had changed, and she would never be the same again.

CHAPTER ELEVEN

CASSIE made the most of her day off, spending it as a lady of leisure, which was an unaccustomed luxury for her these days.

Rising late, she had a long, scented lie-in in the bath, donned one of her ready-made outfits, and took herself round the stores in search of a dress for David and Sarah Hollister's party, to which Justin was taking her to-morrow night.

It was an unnecessary exercise, for her cupboards were stuffed with this season's best from several couturiers, but like women the world over, when she wanted to dress for a special man only a special dress would do.

Not that her purpose was to take Justin's breath away, or his sister's either, for that matter, though she'd relish making that supercilious young woman realise that the female who shared Miles's working life was someone to be reckoned with. No, the object of her attention was Miles himself, who she was pretty sure would be at the party too, with some bewitching lady in tow.

It was late afternoon when she returned home, well satisfied with her purchases, for naturally she hadn't been able to resist buying several outfits that had caught her eye. Tired from her shopping spree—it would be a relief to return to the office!—she went to bed early with the latest bestseller from a rival publishing house, but found the heroine's adventures so dull compared with the in-trigue going on in her own life that she flung it aside and went to sleep.

Arriving at the office, she was put out to find that Miles had gone out of town for the day, not forgetting to leave her a full tape of letters to transcribe! Her typing was now good enough for her to do it herself, but after

tapping away for the entire morning and only com-
pleting a quarter of the work, she sent the rest of the
tape to the bureau.

At five o'clock she went home, and was in the act of
dressing for the Hollisters' party when the doorbell rang.
Switching on the video entry-phone, she made certain it
was Justin before pressing the release catch on the front
door to let him in.

'I won't be long,' she called out. 'Help yourself to a
drink.'

Hurriedly she slipped into silk briefs, then pulled on
cobweb-sheer tights. A ladder sneaked up her calf, and
with an exclamation she rummaged in the drawer for
another pair. When she finally entered the living-room
she was flushed and breathless, and flushed even more
when she saw Justin glancing through her engagement
diary near the telephone.

'If you're curious to know what I'm doing you only
have to ask,' she stated.

'Sorry, angel. I was checking to see if you were free
for the weekend. Wendy and Martin want us to go with
them to the Cotswolds.' He named some friends who
had a cottage near Banbury.

This was the second occasion he had asked her and,
as on the previous occasion, she had no intention of
accepting.

'I'm going out Saturday night,' she said, no need to
mention it was with Miles.

'We can go for the day on Sunday?' he suggested.

'No can do.'

'Are you dating another man?'

'We never agreed exclusive rights,' she hedged.

'I'd be happy to.' He pulled her into his arms and
pressed her against his body, his hands hard as they
moved down her spine to rest on her hips. 'I'm crazy
about you, Cassie. When are you going to take me
seriously?'

'We're late for the party,' she evaded, unwilling to ruin the evening at the outset, but determined to make her position clear when he brought her home.

'We're the least important guests,' he said drily. 'Sarah won't mind if we don't turn up at all.'

'Maybe, but I bought this outfit specially, and I'd like to show it off!'

Reluctantly he let her go, and helped her on with the jacket of her suit—a black wool Ralph Lauren with cream crêpe-de-Chine waterfall revers, the same colour as the chemise top worn beneath; that it was also the same colour as her skin added to the illusion that she was topless—a fact which Justin noted.

'I'm glad you aren't confining those lovely breasts of yours with a bra.'

'I dislike strapless ones,' she shrugged, and reaching for her purse preceded him to the door, anxious to stop any further talk about her body. Yet if the right man had been discussing her breasts she would have taken pleasure in it!

'I've never seen you look so gorgeous,' Justin observed as they drove from the house. 'I bet you didn't get that outfit in a chain store.'

'From a dress agency,' she lied, glad she had prepared an answer to such a question. 'I often go to the same one, and if they get in anything special they give me a call.'

'I guessed it was an original. I've an eye for fashion. Comes from having Sarah as a sister. Clothes are her passion.'

Not the only one, Cassie nearly said, but bit back the words.

'Had a good day?' Justin asked as they entered Regent's Park and headed towards Belgravia.

'Not as hectic as yesterday. I went to New York for the day.'

'*You what?*'

In astonished silence he listened while she recounted her trip and the reason for it.

'You certainly have nerve,' he muttered when she had finished. 'If your gamble hadn't come off Miles wouldn't have reimbursed you for your fare.'

'I never considered failing. From what I'd heard of Seamus O'Mara I knew it was the kind of grandiose gesture to appeal to him.'

A line of cars was already discharging formally attired guests outside the Hollisters' house off Belgrave Square. Their hosts were standing together in the hall, and double doors on either side of them, leading to the drawing and dining-room, were open to allow people to wander freely.

Cassie was dismayed to discover that Sarah was lovelier than she had remembered. Her ash-blonde hair was swept back from a stunningly beautiful face to reveal aquamarine earrings which echoed the greeny-blue of her chiffon dress and her eyes. Slender and petite, with a flawless skin and delicate features, she resembled a Dresden figurine. And as malleable, Cassie thought, noting the firmness of the small mouth. Yet it was easy to understand why, despite walking out on Miles, she still held him in thrall, for she exuded a raw sexuality made all the more intriguing by her fragile demeanour.

She greeted her brother affectionately and Cassie with studied charm, her eyes flickering quickly over the Ralph Lauren dress. I'd never manage to kid *her* I bought it from a dress agency, Cassie thought wryly. She knows it's this season's model, and might even have one in her own wardrobe!

'Do go and have a drink,' Sarah said in her soft, husky voice before turning her attention to the next guests.

Justin guided Cassie into the drawing-room where staff were plying trays of drinks. He helped her to a glass of champagne, then raised his towards her.

'To the loveliest girl I know,' he toasted. 'Can't I persuade you to put off your other date and spend the weekend with me?'

'Naughty, naughty,' she said lightly. 'How would you feel if I broke a date with *you*?'

He made a face, but did not argue, and instead drained his drink. Cassie did the same, and he took the two glasses.

'I'll get refills. Don't wander off or I'll lose you in the crowd.'

He was absent longer than she had expected, and when she finally saw him coming towards her he had another man in tow. Miles. Her heart did a silly flip-flop, then settled to a steady ninety-four! How arresting he was— by far the most stunning man she had ever encountered, though he wasn't conventionally handsome. But then, good looks weren't simply a question of the right features and colouring. Without personality a good-looking man or woman was like a tailor's dummy—an accusation which could never be levelled at Miles!

She had not seen him in a dinner-jacket before, and its impeccable cut and the elegance of the material was in direct contrast to the very male strength of his broad shoulders. The sharp white of a cambric shirt drew attention to his lean, olive-skinned face, in which gleamed silvery-grey eyes that disclosed nothing of his emotions. He had taken a firm brush to his hair, which lay sleek and shiny on his scalp, though as he drew near she noticed an errant strand in the front beginning to fall slightly over his forehead.

'I've brought Miles over to take care of you for a while,' Justin said as the two men came to a stop in front of her.

'Hello, Cassie,' Miles greeted her. 'You never mentioned you'd be here tonight.'

'I didn't get the chance. You were out of the office yesterday.' She glanced at Justin. 'Are you going out, then?'

'I have to take a look at one of Sarah's guests. She's pregnant, and isn't feeling well. I explained that my speciality is babies *outside* the womb, not in it, but if you're a doctor people think you're knowledgeable on *every* medical subject! Miles was close by when Sarah asked me to see the woman, and he offered to take care of you.'

'I'm not a baby,' Cassie said coolly, not relishing the idea of Miles being obliged to come over to her.

'Then perhaps you'll take care of *me* instead?' Miles suggested. 'That way I'll get to stay with the prettiest girl here.'

'Remember you only have temporary custody,' Justin warned. 'I'll be back shortly.'

Leaning forward, he kissed her quickly on the mouth before hurrying off, and Cassie knew it had been a deliberate 'my property' action. She was conscious of Miles watching him go, and wasn't too surprised at his next remark.

'I hadn't realised you and Justin were a twosome.'

'A good-friends-only twosome.'

'How did you meet?'

'At a party.'

'Are you a party girl?'

'Not this kind of party,' she said. 'I prefer them smaller and more intimate.'

'Me too. My favourite kind is a party for two!'

With the other member being Sarah, Cassie thought waspishly, but aloud said, 'Then how come you're here?' As if she didn't know!

'Part business, part friendship,' he replied. 'David's bank helped Barlow's financially a few years ago, when it needed cash for expansion, and we've been on social terms since.' One shoulder rose in a shrug. 'But I had to pass up an opening night at Covent Garden.'

'How strong-minded of you!'

'Not really. We can't always do what we want. I missed David's last two parties for various reasons, and I considered it politic not to miss another.'

He had made no mention of being a long-standing 'friend' of Sarah's, and Cassie played the innocent. 'His wife's very beautiful, isn't she?'

'And a great hostess,' he added, his expression hard to read. 'David's a lucky man. She fits into his lifestyle as to the manner born. When his elderly bachelor cousin dies she'll be Lady Hollister, and all her dreams will have come true.'

But what of Miles's dreams? Cassie wondered. Was he happy to accept what Sarah was willing to give him? The thought of him indulging in a secret affair with her, while continuing his friendship with her husband, filled Cassie with disgust, and with anger for herself because knowing what he was doing made no difference to what she felt for him.

She inched back from him, but the faint scent of his aftershave lingered in her nostrils. It was astringent, with an underlying musky warmth, like the man himself, for he could be both sharp and charming, using either aspect of his character to help him get what he wanted. And how easily he could get *her*, if he set his mind to it. Frightened by the depth of her longing for him, she went on the attack.

'Weren't you and Mrs Hollister a close twosome for many years?' she said boldly.

Miles stood motionless. 'When we were both young and foolish,' he replied flatly. 'Before either of us knew what we really wanted.'

'You still don't seem to know.'

'Because I haven't married, you mean?'

She nodded, and at the same time helped herself to another glass of champagne from a passing waiter.

'Marriage isn't necessarily a pathway to heaven,' Miles went on.

'But it's the road most men take, if only to perpetuate themselves,' Cassie said, thinking of the father she had never met.

'I'd never marry for the sake of having children.'

'You do like them, though?'

'Yes. And also animals and old people,' he smiled. 'I'm not a monster, you know, even if I appear to be one in the office.'

'A dragon breathing fire is a better description!'

'Fortunately, you can take the heat!'

Before she had a chance to answer Justin reappeared. 'Sorry, pet, but I think Sarah's friend is having a miscarriage. I've ordered an ambulance, but she's asked me to go with her to the hospital.'

'Don't worry about Cassie,' Miles interjected. 'I'll see she gets home safely.'

'I hope I'll be back long before then.' He knuckled Cassie's cheek. 'If I'm delayed for any reason I'll call you in the morning.'

'There's no necessity for you to act as my keeper,' Cassie said to Miles as Justin departed. 'I can easily take a taxi home.'

'And I can easily take you in my car. I'm here alone. The girl I was bringing let me down at the last moment.'

'I'm sure it wasn't because she found something better to do,' Cassie retorted.

'So am I,' he agreed smoothly. 'She has flu.'

He sipped his whisky and appraised her over the rim of the glass. She had taken off her jacket, and was aware of not wearing anything beneath her camisole top; aware, too, that because of his height he was able to look down and have a good view of her naked breasts. Not normally shy, she was suddenly overcome with embarrassment, and pulled back her shoulders in an attempt to tighten the neckline.

Amusement lifted the corners of his mouth. 'You have lovely breasts, Cassie. Don't be ashamed of showing them.'

'I'm not,' she denied, her cheeks hot. 'But it depends on the time and the place.'

'How about in our own time at my place?'

Her eyes widened with shock, but his remained steady, and it was impossible to tell if he was serious.

'You once informed me you didn't mix business with pleasure,' she managed to say.

'It's easy to forget that when you look so desirable.'

A tremor went through her, and she felt her breasts harden. 'I'd have thought you were used to desirable women.'

'I'm used to beautiful ones, which isn't necessarily the same thing. You'd be surprised how difficult it is to find a genuinely desirable one—and by that I mean a woman with brains as well as beauty.'

Cassie was sceptical, and, though she did not say so, her face gave her away.

'You don't believe me, do you?'

'Well, let's say your line isn't exactly original,' she stated drily.

'What do you expect? I'm a publisher, not a writer!'

'And I'm your secretary, not a girlfriend. That's why I can distinguish fact from fiction!'

He laughed outright. 'You can dampen a man's ardour with words better than an ice-cold shower!'

'Does that mean you accept defeat?'

'Of course. And we both lose out!'

Cassie relaxed. It was clear he was teasing her and enjoying it.

'Miles! I wondered where you were hiding.'

The voice was Sarah's, and he half turned, disclosing the slender figure in aquamarine. A pale hand, red-tipped, linked itself through his arm, and he imperceptibly stiffened, making Cassie feel he was irritated by Sarah's proprietorial manner, or worried lest David see it.

'Well, now you've found me,' he said calmly, 'what can I do for you?'

'Circulate, darling. I'm sure Cassie won't object.' Sarah gave her a wide smile, her blue eyes blank. 'Anyway, Justin will be back soon.'

She went to draw Miles away, but he resisted. 'Later, Sarah. Cassie and I are going to get some food.' Gently he removed the red-tipped fingers linked round his arm, placed his hand beneath Cassie's elbow, and propelled her towards the buffet.

'That wasn't very polite,' Cassie remarked.

'I know.'

His mouth clamped shut, and she wondered if his rudeness had been a display of independence. Perhaps he and Sarah had quarrelled and he was showing her he was still angry. Or perhaps—wonderful thought—he was tiring of their affair. This could explain his attention to herself, for how better to show indifference to one woman than to appear interested in another?

'I'm not very hungry,' she murmured, irritated by the notion that she was being used. 'I'd rather go home.'

'It's far too early.'

'*You're* not suffering from jet lag.'

'Neither are you, so don't give me that! Though you'll be suffering from anorexia if you don't eat.' Handing her a plate, he began piling it with food.

It was lavish and excellent, but she was in no mood to enjoy it, and pushed it round her plate. Miles had no such problems, and attacked his lobster salad with gusto.

'You aren't annoyed with Sarah for trying to prise me from you, are you?' he asked unexpectedly.

'Why should I be? She was right. We aren't a couple, and an unattached man at a party should circulate.'

'Rubbish. You met Justin at a party, and if he'd followed his sister's dictum you wouldn't now be "good friends"!'

'That was different. He was a stranger to me then, but you're my boss.'

'All the more reason for me to be nice to you. Good secretaries are hard to find!'

He probably meant it, too, she thought irritably, yet recollecting he had had no hesitation in firing her over the Seamus affair she decided he was teasing again. Perhaps he was beginning to see her as a person in her own right after all. The possibility was enough to restore her appetite, and she nibbled at a chicken leg.

'These caterers are the best in London,' Miles observed, setting his plate aside.

'All professional catering has the same stamp to it,' she stated, for no other reason than to be contrary. 'I prefer home cooking.'

'That's because you're a good cook.'

He should only know! With assumed modesty she lowered her eyes.

'I must put your culinary prowess to the test,' he continued. 'I've an idea it will be quite an experience.'

That was an understatement! Cassie wished she had told him the truth regarding the cookery books, but it was too late now.

'Don't get carried away,' she said. 'I'm really not that good.'

'Let me be the judge of that.' His voice was warm. 'Why don't we have dinner at your place tomorrow night, instead of going out? I was going to take you to Le Gavroche,' he named one of the capital's finest restaurants, 'but we'll go another time.'

'I'd rather go tomorrow,' she pleaded. Having agreed to go out with him she could hardly cry off now with an excuse. 'I've heard a lot about it, and no one else I know can afford to take me there.'

'We'll go one night next week,' he pacified. 'I'll check my diary to see when I'm free.'

'We might not be able to agree on an evening,' she said hurriedly.

'Don't you wish to cook dinner for me?' he quizzed.

'Of course I do. But I—I'm having trouble with my oven, and I'm not sure if I can use it.'

'I'll send Jack over in the morning to examine it. As a handyman he's a wizard.'

If only he were wizard enough to turn her into an instant gourmet cook! Cassie bit back a sigh. In trying to extricate herself from a hole, she was now in a bigger one. She'd have to phone the chauffeur first thing in the morning and say the oven had suddenly righted itself.

'You're taking your life in your hands,' she warned Miles.

'And placing my stomach in *yours*!'

'Too true. Bring a bottle of Alka-Seltzer. You might need it!'

'I'll bring a bottle of champagne instead—and, of course, I'll reimburse you for the food.'

'There's no need,' she protested.

'If that's true I must be overpaying you!'

Although she made a joking response, she was vaguely worried by his insistence on spending tomorrow evening at her home. She wasn't naïve enough to believe his sole reason was his interest in tasting her cooking, and if he made an attempt to seduce her she was by no means sure she had the will-power to resist him. The fear of giving in to a man was new to her; until today she had found it no hardship to say no, for she abhorred loveless passion. But what she felt for Miles was deeper than anything she had experienced before, and she was scared of being used and discarded by him—which was his usual form.

Yet if he was trying to break from Sarah, then here was her golden opportunity. Sipping her champagne, she studied him beneath her lashes. He had undone his jacket, and she glimpsed the darkness of the hair on his chest through the fine white cambric of his shirt. Hastily she lowered her eyes to the royal blue cummerbund around his waist. It lent him a dashing, buccaneering air that went well with his assertive manner. Was that how he'd be as a lover—demanding and positive, taking what he wanted when it suited him? Or would he be gentle and considerate, willing to wait until they both reached the same peak of arousal, and could climax together?

Her body trembled, heat coursing through her as tormenting images of Miles with other women filled her mind. It was incomprehensible to her that Sarah countenanced his stream of girlfriends. Or did his having them make her life easier? After all, a man whose passion was partially appeased was easier to pacify, and, considering she had to play her part as the perfect wife and was not always available for him, this might be a relief to her.

The sight of David Hollister coming towards her was a welcome distraction to Cassie. When they had last met in Miles's office he had been friendly and had spoken of Justin, intimating that he knew she was seeing his brother-in-law—unlike his wife, who had given no indication of it.

'Sorry to hear Justin had to dash off,' he said in his smooth, quiet voice. 'But I see Miles is entertaining you. At least I hope he is, and not giving you a list of instructions of what to do on Monday!'

'I'm not quite such a taskmaster,' Miles reproved. 'Actually, I was chatting her up!'

'Then I'm doubly sorry for having to take you away for a short while. But Sir Leon Pakard has dropped in for a drink, and wishes to have a word with you. He's still interested in acquiring that property.'

Miles flung Cassie an apologetic glance. 'I won't be long.'

'Don't worry, I'll be fine.'

As he moved off, Cassie searched and found an empty chair in an alcove behind a floor-standing urn filled with flowers. She had a view of the room through the foliage, yet was partially hidden, which gave her the opportunity of going over what Miles had said and, equally important, to ponder how much of it he had meant.

CHAPTER TWELVE

CASSIE was given no time to think about Miles, for hardly had she made herself comfortable than she was joined by her hostess. Quite evidently the woman had eagle eyes, and had been watching her all the time she was with Miles.

'Justin told me of your trip to New York,' Sarah said. 'No wonder you look tired.'

'I was hoping it didn't show.' Cassie hid a smile at the obvious manner in which her hostess was trying to put her down.

'I'm afraid it does,' came the blunt reply. 'Though maybe it's also the strain of working for Miles. I believe he can be very demanding.'

'But he gives back such a lot, too,' Cassie enthused. 'I'm gaining a great insight into the mechanics of publishing.'

'Really? I'd better warn Miles to watch out for his job!'

'He encourages me to take an interest in the company,' Cassie said deliberately. 'That way he can talk things over with me.'

Once again Sarah's mouth tightened. 'I've often regretted giving up my career, but David frequently travels abroad and likes me to go with him.'

'How do you fill in the rest of your time?'

'I do charity work, and run our homes.'

They had three, but no children, and Cassie wondered why. She made a mental note to find out from Justin.

'What did you do before you were married?' she questioned instead, hoping Sarah would refer to her years with Miles.

'I was with Anglia Television. But then I met Miles and moved to Oxford to be with him. He was a brilliant lecturer, and students queued to hear him speak. He loved every minute of it, and never contemplated any other life.'

'Oxford's a lovely place,' Cassie murmured, hoping to encourage further confidences.

'I prefer London or Paris.' A slim hand languidly waved the air. 'And academic life is narrow and boring—unless you're an academic, which I'm not. I was ready to climb up the wall when David came on the scene, and I realised my feelings for Miles had changed.' Sarah half turned in her chair to regard Cassie fully. 'He was devastated, of course. Begged me not to leave him—even offered to move to London and find other work, but I wouldn't let him. I didn't think he'd be happy away from his students and the university.'

It wasn't quite the same story as Justin's, but Cassie appreciated why, for this version put Sarah in a far better light. To leave one man because she had fallen for another was less reprehensible than leaving him solely for material reasons.

'You must have been astonished when Miles opted for a career in publishing,' she said, careful to show no bias in her tone.

'I was. And I'm thrilled he's successful at it. Of course, I'd be much happier if he were married—I'd feel less guilty for leaving him—but I'm afraid he hasn't stopped loving me. That's why he plays the field, you know.' A slim hand moved again, but this time to rest on Cassie's arm. 'Oh, dear, I'm not usually indiscreet. Please forget I said that.'

'It's forgotten,' Cassie assured her, fully aware that the indiscretion was intentional. 'I make it a habit never to remember gossip.'

Sarah rose, the flush on her alabaster skin showing that the rebuff was not lost on her. 'I hope Miles appreciates what a treasure he has for a secretary,' she said, and drifted away on a cloud of Valentino chiffon and Giorgio perfume.

Once again Cassie was alone with her thoughts, and once again she was not left to them, for a tall, spare man with dark hair and greying sideburns introduced himself with a slight bow.

'I am Jacques Fourrier.' His voice had the lilting cadence of the French. 'I'm with David's bank.'

'And I'm with David's brother-in-law,' she answered lightly.

'Not for the rest of the evening, I understand. I heard he has taken one of the guests to hospital.' Dark eyes ranged over her body, pausing momentarily on the creamy cleavage. 'But I hope his loss will be my gain. I wanted to come over as soon as he left, but Miles beat me to it.'

'I work for him.'

'Lucky Miles to have such a beautiful associate.'

'Hardly an associate. I'm his secretary.'

'Whatever you are, I'm sure you're a treasure.' The Frenchman's glance was frank. 'May I sit with you?' The question was rhetorical, for he didn't wait for a reply before taking the chair vacated by Sarah. 'It's easier to talk on the same level, even if the view isn't as interesting!'

There was no doubting his meaning, and for the second time that evening Cassie felt herself redden.

It was not lost on the Frenchman. 'How delightful that in this day of topless, bottomless and wantonness one can find a young woman who can still blush! You must tell me all about yourself.'

'I already have. I work for Barlow's.'

'That's only the beginning. I want to know more about you. Where do you live?'

'Camden Town.'

'Alone?'

'Yes.'

'Does that mean you and the doctor are merely friends?'

'It means I prefer to live alone.'

He chuckled. 'Quick-witted too. How long have you worked for Miles?'

'It's my turn to ask a question,' she smiled, anxious to divert his attention away from her. 'How long have you lived in England?'

'Three years.'

'Is your wife at the party?' Cassie had noticed his gold wedding-ring, and hoped her question would put an end to his compliments.

'No, she's in Lyons visiting her parents,' he replied blandly. 'My days are busy, so I don't miss her, but the nights are cold and lonely. Have you any suggestions?'

'Buy an electric blanket and a dog!'

'You're sharp,' he smiled. 'But then you would have to be, working for Miles. He dislikes mediocrity.'

She nodded. 'I've never met anyone with a keener brain. He——'

'I'm aware of his qualities. Our bank wouldn't have helped Barlow's if he hadn't been running it.'

'I thought Henry Barlow ran it with him,' Cassie said carefully.

'In the beginning. But for the last six years Barlow's has been Miles's.'

'Really?'

'Assuredly.' Jacques Fourrier spread his hands. 'He is a person who can take over any company and set it to rights. And people of that calibre are few and far between. In my opinion he will go on to bigger and better things.'

Cassie didn't like the sound of this. 'I don't think that's Miles's aim. He's very happy where he is.'

'For the moment.'

'You're thinking of Catherine Barlow, I assume?' Cassie queried.

'Yes. No one knows what her plans are.' The Frenchman shrugged. 'But enough talk of others. It's you I am interested in. Are you free to dine with me tomorrow?'

'I already have a date. I'm busy the whole weekend, in fact, and next week too,' she added, having no intention of going out with a married man.

'I'm not surprised.' Lightly he stroked her arm. 'Say the week after next?'

'I try not to make arrangements too far ahead. I often work late, you see.'

'Working late at the office is usually the man's line!'

'Don't you mean the husband's?' she replied succinctly.

'Sorry to break up your tête-à-tête.' Miles interposed, appearing without warning. 'I'm ready to take you home, Cassie, if you want to go.'

She jumped up with relief, and Jacques Fourrier rose with her.

'It's no wonder she's tired, Miles,' he said smoothly. 'She's been telling me of the long hours you work her.'

'And also that I love every minute of it,' Cassie interjected, liking her new acquaintance less and less.

Miles placed a firm hand on her bare back, and, with a cool goodnight to the other man, led her away.

'I take it you wanted to leave with me?' he asked as the front door closed behind them.

'What should you think otherwise?'

He stopped beside his dark green Daimler and unlocked the doors. 'You appeared to be getting on well together, and I thought you might have preferred him to take you home.'

'He happens to be married.'

'Sorry,' he said, not sounding it. 'I didn't realise your middle name was Purity.'

'There's no reason to be sarcastic,' she snapped. '*You* may think it old-fashioned of me, but that's how I feel.'

Before she had finished speaking, she wished the words unsaid, for her comment could easily be taken as a dig at him. After all, Sarah's car had been prominently displayed outside his house the night she had delivered the manuscript to him. But short of apologising there was nothing she could do, and silently she took her place beside him in the car.

They drove in silence, and she stared intently through the window, as if she had never seen Hyde Park before.

'You certainly gave the impression you liked him.' Miles spoke again, and on the same subject, which irritated her.

'I was simply being civil.'

'I suppose you were simply being civil in allowing a man you'd just met to maul you.'

'I'd hardly call a hand on my arm mauling! But what do you think I should have done? Slapped his face?'

'You must have encouraged him,' Miles grunted.

'Men don't need encouragement to make a pass,' she retorted. 'But what business is it of yours, anyway? You aren't my keeper.'

'Perhaps I'd like to be.'

The car stopped as abruptly as his sentence, and her seatbelt jerked her violently back. Angrily she swung round on him.

'What's that supposed to mean?'

'I want to make love to you, and I can't stand anyone else touching you.'

She was digesting this when he slid across the seat, pressing her body back against the car door.

'You've bewitched me,' he said huskily, then his head blotted out the dim glow that came from the dashboard as his lips pressed hungrily on hers. 'I've wanted you for weeks,' he muttered against them. 'God, how I've wanted you.'

The urgency of his need was apparent, not only through his voice and the pressure of his mouth, but also the trembling movements of his hands as they glided over her breasts and down her spine. Fluidly, and without pause, he lowered the zip of her dress and began caressing the naked flesh.

Cassie gasped and tried to draw away, but the parting of her lips inflamed him further, and his tongue probed the inner softness.

'You're beautiful,' he said thickly, lowering his head to place his lips upon one rose-pink nipple, and feathering it with light, quick kisses.

Again she tried to pull back from him, unnerved by the intensity of her response. She wanted Miles as much as he wanted her—wanted him close, to go on kissing and caressing her, wanting the exploration of his hands that aroused an agony of weakness which made her feel as if her entire body were floating on a sea of desire. A convulsive tremor made her quiver in his arms, and the softness of her breasts swelled and hardened, as his own body was hardening.

'Cassie,' he murmured, drawing a nipple deep into his mouth, each sweep of his tongue bringing a new assault on her senses.

'Miles, don't,' she cried. 'Please don't.'

'I'd never force you,' he whispered, moving away from her.

His tone was steady, but in the dimness of the car she discerned the glitter of passion in the narrowed eyes. Meeting them, she shivered at what she saw there: a raw desire that made her all too aware of her nakedness and vulnerability.

With trembling fingers she raised the zip of her dress and pulled her jacket around her. Every pore in her body seemed to be alive, every nerve in her tingling.

'Forgive me, Cassie. I'm sorry,' he said jerkily. 'I don't know what came over me.'

'I think it's called lust,' she replied, surprised that her voice gave no indication of the turmoil within her.

'You're very desirable, Cassie.' His voice was still thick, indicating his emotions were far from under control. 'But until tonight I hadn't realised I was so susceptible.'

'Thanks for not insinuating I encouraged you,' she said scathingly.

He shifted, and ran a finger round the rim of his collar. 'I apologise for that remark about Jacques. Put it down to jealousy.'

'Does lust qualify you to be jealous of me?'

'You've every right to be angry,' he conceded quietly. 'There's no way to explain my behaviour, and I promise it won't happen again, so you needn't sit there trying to work out how you're going to tell me you're leaving!'

Nothing had been further from her mind but, realising that under normal circumstances it would have been an obvious reaction, she played along with it. 'How clever of you to guess. You must be psychic.'

He shrugged. 'It's the reaction I'd expect, given our working relationship and the embarrassment you think it might cause.'

'*You* made the rules against fraternisation,' she reminded him again.

'Because I fancied you the minute I saw you,' he admitted.

'I suppose I should be flattered?'

'Clearly you're not.'

Cassie hesitated, not certain where the truth lay. Part of her was pleased—all women enjoyed knowing they were desired—but the other part, the one that needed emotional involvement, had left her feeling used.

'Don't bother replying,' he said abruptly, and switched on the engine. 'You've made the answer plain.'

If his driving was anything to go by he had completely recovered his equilibrium, the steady speed indicative of passion cooled. How easily he could switch off, she thought, and wished she had the same facility. Her limbs still trembled, and the innermost part of her pulsated from the touch of his hands, the feel of his mouth. She had been kissed many times by men handsomer than Miles. But never had they aroused such conflicting emotions in her. Never had she been so uncertain of what she wanted.

Cassie glanced at him. 'Perhaps it might be better if we went to Le Gavroche for dinner tomorrow night, after all?'

'A woman only has to turn me down once,' he said softly. 'I never try a second time.'

'Supposing we were marooned on a desert island?' she asked facetiously.

'I'd hope it was near the Arctic.'

'Why?'

'There'd be no shortage of cold showers!'

She laughed, and slid out of the car. 'Goodnight, Miles. See you tomorrow.' But as she reached the front door she found him towering beside her in the darkness.

'Scared you might be tempted to say "yes" if I don't keep my distance?' he mocked.

It was too near the truth for comfort. 'Why should you try to take a girl who's resisted you, when you know masses who wouldn't?' she retorted.

A laugh rumbled in his throat. 'Because you're spunky and never short of an answer. That's one of the things I like about you.' He ran a finger lightly along her cheekbone. 'One of the many things.' Bending his head, he softly kissed her brow. 'Goodnight, Miss Spitfire, sleep well.'

She was entering her bedroom when she heard his car drive away, and, even when she could no longer hear the sound of it, it remained in her imagination as she pictured him driving through the darkness, their encounter dismissed, his thoughts centred on other things. It was a facility she envied—an ability to compartmentalise his mind, to concentrate on what he considered to be important, and dismiss the inconsequential. Since none of his relationships with women lasted long, they obviously fell into this category.

As hers would if she decided to see him socially. After all, he wasn't interested in a relationship—only sex. He had not pretended otherwise. Yet had he done, she would have considered him a hypocrite. So why was she angry with him? Was it because she had fallen in love with him? She tossed her head. Heavens! She wasn't even sure she liked him. Yet 'like' often had nothing to do with love, for love could be illogical and inexplicable.

'I can't be in love with him!' she denied aloud. 'It's impossible.'

But it wasn't. It was a fact.

'I can't be,' she denied again, and marched into the kitchen to fix herself a hot drink. How could she have given her heart to a man who shied away from permanent relationships, and had no wish for long-term commitment? He wanted to go to bed with her and, more important, respected her intelligence—a rare occurrence for him, he had said. While this might mean that if she had an affair with him it could last longer than most, it didn't signify marriage. And, for the first time, she had met a man with whom she wanted to share her life.

Cupping her hands round a mug of hot milk, she curled up in a chair in the living-room. What did she know of Miles other than what she had gleaned from gossip, and the few things he had let slip? He had three sisters, all married, and his parents had retired to Aix en Provence. On the odd occasion when he mentioned his family it was with affection, and she knew he flew down to see his parents every few months. Comfortably off rather than rich, Miles had come from a privileged background of public school and Oxford, and had no need to prove himself, as was often the case with ambitious men.

What had driven him to leave the academic life he loved and enter the commercial rat race? How to explain the single-minded attachment to work that left him no inclination to share his life with a woman?

One name answered both questions. Sarah. If he was still carrying the torch for her it explained everything. For what better way of showing her that, had she stayed with him, he could have given her the same lifestyle as the man she had left him for?

Despondently Cassie set down the mug, and went to bed. Should she try to fight for Miles, or was it better to fight her love for him? She was still mulling over the problem when she fell asleep.

CHAPTER THIRTEEN

BY THE following morning Cassie had formulated a plan to deceive Miles. Given that her culinary skills didn't go beyond toast and scrambled eggs there was no way she could prepare the kind of meal he was expecting.

But even if she knew nothing of preparing food her knowledge and appreciation of it was in the gourmet category, and she knew exactly the sort of meal she wanted to serve.

First she had to call Miles to tell him her oven had miraculously righted itself.

'It must have been a fuse,' she said. 'My washing-machine's on the same plug, and when it didn't work this morning I changed it, and the oven clock started. So I'll expect you at seven-thirty.'

'Shall I come along earlier to help?' he offered.

'Thanks, but it's all in hand.'

At least it soon would be, she vowed as she set off for Hampstead High Street, though at the moment it was all in the shops!

Browsing round several delicatessens, she found one that fulfilled most of her requirements, and waited in the queue to be served.

'Been here before?' the woman in front of her asked conversationally.

'No,' Cassie replied. 'But everything looks delicious.'

'It is. That's why they're so busy. Half of Hampstead come here on the cook's night out, and the other half when they're giving a dinner party—unless they're inviting guests who live locally, of course. Then they'd recognise the food!'

Cassie's heart sank. This might well apply to Miles, and there was no way she dared run the risk.

Murmuring that she didn't have time to wait, she left the shop. What to do now? Go to Selfridges or Harrods, or see if she could order a meal from a restaurant? Not just any restaurant, though. She'd order it from Le Gavroche! She chuckled, enjoying the irony of serving a meal bought from the very restaurant Miles had proposed taking her to. The chef proprietor knew her parents well and, amused by her predicament, agreed to help her.

With the promise that the food would be delivered to her by five, she returned home laden with flowers, arranged them artistically in vases round the living-room, set the table, and then, with no sense of guilt whatever, settled back on the sofa to watch a video film.

At five o'clock she was waiting expectantly for the taxi to arrive with the food, and when five-thirty came and went she telephoned the restaurant.

'We put the food into a taxi more than an hour ago,' a waiter informed her. 'Perhaps it was involved in an accident.'

Cassie clutched at the receiver. 'Can you send me a repeat order right away? I'll pay you for both, of course.'

'The kitchen is busy preparing the evening's dinners, and we couldn't dispatch anything until after seven.'

Cassie's heart thumped painfully in her chest. What egg she'd have on her face if the food and Miles arrived on her doorstep at the same time! Murmuring that seven was too late, she hung up. She would have to phone Miles and plead illness. A migraine maybe. No, he might come round with some tablets. A stomach upset was better. She was reaching for the telephone when the doorbell rang, and through the living-room window she glimpsed the square bulk of a taxi.

With a sigh of relief, she rushed to the door. 'Thank goodness you've arrived!'

'Terribly sorry, miss,' the taxi-driver apologised, setting a large insulated box on the floor. 'I had a puncture, and my spare was flat too! I hope I'm not too late?'

'Not at all,' Cassie said with a brilliant smile, and, giving him a more than generous payment, carried the box into the kitchen and carefully transferred the food to her own serving dishes.

The restaurant had given careful thought to what they had sent her. Both the first and last course were cold, and the main one was sufficiently under-cooked not to be spoilt by heating in her microwave. There was even a selection of wonderful cheeses, for which she sent up a prayer of thanks. If Miles didn't have a sweet tooth she'd have been in trouble.

Happily she went to change. She wanted to look a knock-out, yet knowing the danger inherent in that— Miles might think it a come-on—she opted for the softly feminine: a flowing crêpe silk skirt in the deep purple of African violets, with a rose crêpe top whose gently scooped neckline gave only a slight glimpse of shadowed cleavage. She wore the minimum of make-up, for excitement had given a sparkle to her eyes and a bloom to her skin, and she left her gleaming chestnut hair loose and flowing to her shoulders.

As the time of Miles's arrival drew near Cassie moved restlessly round the room, straightening a cushion, moving a vase, checking to see she had put out a bowl of nuts and crisps, and had a bottle of wine in the refrigerator, in case he had forgotten he had said he would bring one.

I've done him an injustice, she thought as his car drew up outside and, peeping through the window, she watched him walk up the narrow paved path holding a bottle of champagne and a small, beribboned package. For a moment after he rang the bell she waited, then sauntered to the front door and opened it.

As always at close range, his charisma overwhelmed her, and she had to make a conscious effort not to catch her breath. He was formally dressed in a lightweight grey suit that was the identical colour of his eyes—when he was in a good temper. And he was in a very good temper at this moment, for they were the grey of woodland smoke. But, as a concession to a warm summer's evening and the fact that they were dining at home, he wore no tie and his pale blue shirt was open at the throat.

'For you,' he said, handing her the champagne and the package.

'How extravagant of you,' she murmured, running her finger across the label on the bottle. 'I wasn't anticipating vintage Dom Perignon.'

'A lady as beautiful and intelligent as you should only expect the best.'

Head tilted, her eyes went from him to the gift-wrapped package. 'What's this for?'

'A thank-you for the wonderful meal I'm going to have! I know flowers or chocolates are the usual thing, but I wanted to give you something you'd keep.'

Smiling, she led the way into the living-room, the package balanced in her hand. It was light, and her first guess was that it was a piece of jewellery. Had he actually bought it for her, or did he keep a stock of gifts to hand out to his passing girlfriends? Hastily she banished the unpleasant thought.

'Aren't you going to open it?' he prompted.

'I'll put the champagne in the refrigerator first.'

'It's already cold.'

'Like me,' she smiled. 'I hope you aren't expecting to warm me up later?'

'Banish such suspicious thoughts,' he replied, skilfully uncorking the champagne and filling the two glasses she had earlier set out on a tray. 'I'm here for the food, and have no appetite for anything else!' He raised his glass and touched it to hers. 'Here's to a memorable evening.'

Cassie took a generous swallow, and gave an appreciative murmur, then set down her glass to undo her gift. The wrapping fell away to reveal a plain white box. Lifting the lid, she saw a beautifully painted glass bottle about two inches high, with a tiny ivory spoon attached to the inside of the stopper. She assumed it was for scent,

but the spoon puzzled her, and she decided to play safe
in the hope that he would enlighten her.

'It's beautiful, Miles. Really beautiful.'

'You said you couldn't afford to collect snuff bottles,
so I thought it might be a nice idea to start you off with
one.'

That explained the tiny spoon! It was for taking the
snuff out of the bottle in order to sniff it. Given the
Chinese-style decoration of trees and flowers in shades
of bright blue, green and coral, it was stupid of her not
to have connected it with her so-called hobby.

'Where did you find it?' she asked.

'I rang the Chinese department at the Victoria and
Albert Museum, and they told me where to go.'

It was difficult not to be impressed by the trouble he
had gone to, and she wondered at the motive behind it.
Perhaps there wasn't one, and she was looking for
gremlins unnecessarily.

'I really appreciate it, Miles. I'll give it a place of
honour so everyone can admire it.' She put it on the top
of the bookshelf. 'Will you excuse me for a moment while
I check the dinner?'

'What delightful concoctions are you serving?' he
smiled.

'I'd rather surprise you.'

He followed her into the kitchen, and watched as she
put the finishing touches to the green salad—the only
thing she had prepared herself. The dressing was from
a local shop, and luckily she had put it into a sauce-boat
of her own.

'If this is any indication, I can see I'm in for a treat,'
he said as he dipped his finger into the dressing and tasted
it.

'Would you mind taking it in?' she requested. 'And
I'll follow with the hors d'oeuvre.'

They ate their meal at the small dining-room table,
placed at one end of the living-room. Candles flickered
in silver holders, reflecting tiny pin-points of light in the

crystal goblets and the green and gold edges of the Crown Derby china.

'This is superb,' Miles said as he finished the last mouthful of lightly poached crayfish on a bed of saffron sauce, garnished with tiny slivers of cucumber and tomato. 'It must have taken hours to prepare.'

'It's easier than it looks,' she said modestly.

The main course of fillet of lamb with parsley and garlic cream aroused even more wonderment, and the raspberry soufflé dessert was praised with equal enthusiasm.

'We wouldn't have had a better meal at Le Gavroche,' he commented as he relaxed on the settee with a coffee.

'How sweet of you to say that,' she cooed. 'But I think you're exaggerating.'

'I'm not. You're good enough to open a restaurant. Ever thought of it?'

'Never,' she stated so firmly that he looked at her with surprise. 'I—er—I mean I couldn't afford it.'

'I'd be happy to back you.'

Did he mean it, or was he flattering her to disarm her? Cassie nibbled her lower lip nervously. It might have been wiser to have bought everything from a Chinese take-away!

'I'd be frightened of the responsibility,' she said, taking no chances. 'Anyway, I enjoy my present job! And talking of jobs, how did you meet Henry Barlow?'

'He was given an honorary degree at the university where I was lecturing. Afterwards we started chatting, and he seemed to like my ideas. He asked me up to London, offered me a job, and the rest, as they say, is history!'

'Are all your family as successful?'

'In their own way. My father is retired, as you know, and my three sisters elected to devote their energies to their children.' A tender look crossed his face. 'I have eleven nieces and nephews, and when we all get together it's chaos. Fortunately it doesn't happen too often.' He spoke with affection, and it was evident he was joking.

'Coming from an obviously happy family, I'm surprised you're still single,' Cassie said in a matter-of-fact tone.

'Perhaps I haven't met the right woman.'

'Have you ever had a long-term relationship—other than with Sarah?' she asked, greatly daring.

'No—but lately I've been tempted.'

Cassie's pulses quickened. 'Do I know the lucky girl?'

'You should do—it's you,' he said huskily, and, pulling her into his arms, gently pressed her down on the couch.

His mouth fastened on hers, and it was difficult to believe that lips that could look so hard could kiss with such tenderness. Cassie felt as if she was drowning in his hold as the pressure of his body pinned her against the cushions, and all the while his mouth was cajoling her with infinite patience into a response she did not want to give, but was finding increasingly difficult to withhold.

Desire fought with fear, and desire won as she abandoned herself to his touch, opening her arms to clasp him closer, her body relaxing the better to feel him, her lips parting to absorb the warm intimacy of his tongue. Deeper and deeper he invaded her, until her limbs were ablaze with the need of him, and passion burned away logic until she was on fire for him. Expertly his hands slid beneath her skirt, stroking curving thighs, moving over silken-skinned stomach, each caress increasing the throbbing urgency within her. But as a hand lowered she gave a cry and pushed him away.

'Why?' he asked in a low voice, face flushed, breathing fast. 'You want me as much as I want you.'

'That's beside the point,' she said angrily. 'You promised you wouldn't try anything. If I'd thought otherwise I wouldn't have invited you here.'

'I can't fathom why you're making such a fuss. We're both adult, and we're both free. So why——?'

'I'm not interested in joining the queue.'

'How do you know the queue wouldn't end with *you*?'

For several seconds she regarded him. There was no expression on his face, no movement of any of its muscles to give away his thoughts. She longed to believe what he was implying, but didn't trust her judgement. Worse still, she didn't trust *him*.

Common sense told her he saw her as he saw all women—as fair game. He had realised where he had gone wrong last time, and rethought his strategy. She was a conquest to him, nothing more, and if he had to pretend emotions for her that he didn't feel in order to get her, then he'd do so.

'I thought a long-term relationship went against the rules you made for yourself,' she said flatly.

'There are exceptions to every rule!'

'I've no desire to be the latest in a long line of exceptions!' she retorted.

Their eyes met and held—hers sherry-brown and defiant, his silver-grey and determined.

'I mean it, Miles. If you won't take no for an answer, I'll leave you.'

'That's hitting below the belt! It's easier to replace a girlfriend than a good secretary—and, as I've told you before, you're the best I've had.'

'Thanks,' she managed to say, despising herself for loving him when he so patently only saw her as a sex-object.

'Don't be annoyed with me for trying again,' he said. 'You're a beautiful woman, and any man worth his salt would have done the same.'

It wasn't exactly an apology, but Cassie accepted it as such because it suited her to do so. She had come to London for a purpose, and though the purpose had changed—something which she had only just realised—she wasn't quite ready to show her hand.

He didn't linger, nor had she expected him to, and she silently saw him to the door, closing it even before he reached his car. What a sour end to what had begun as a sweet evening.

Whoever said falling in love was wonderful? Possibly it was if the feeling was reciprocated, but in her case it was agony. It would take all her strength of character to continue seeing him every day and pretend indifference. Each new girlfriend of his would be another twist to the knife embedded in her heart.

How would he react when he finally learned she was Catherine Barlow? Would he be furious, or would she be able to make him see she had only embarked on her subterfuge because he would never willingly have taught her how to run Barlow's?

Yet as of this moment her plans had changed drastically. So drastically that she was amazed at herself.

She had promised Lionel Newman to make Miles a partner, and so keep the pledge her natural father had made but not fulfilled. But now she was going to do far more. She would give him half her shares and put him in sole charge of the company. Then she would return to New York and pick up the pieces of her life. She had done everything possible to encourage him to fall in love with her, and if he still only regarded her as a bed playmate, then to hell with him.

This decision made, she felt as if a weight had lifted from her.

CHAPTER FOURTEEN

NEXT morning Cassie had changed her mind. Not about putting Miles in sole charge of Barlow's—that was immutable—but about returning to New York.

Dammit, she was in love with the man! She couldn't give up on him without a fight. From now on she'd be less sarcastic with him and more meltingly feminine; if she could encourage him to feel tenderness towards her, as well as desire, it might lower his defences.

Miles was not in the office when she arrived there on Monday morning. He was having a breakfast meeting with their printers, but was due back by ten to see Clive Gordon, head of the advertising agency who handled their account. She had often spoken to him on the telephone, but they had never met, and she was pleasantly surprised to find he was in his early thirties and very attractive.

He was equally taken with her, as his opening remark signified. 'If I'd known you were as beautiful as your voice I'd have come over sooner!'

Cassie's mouth tilted, but her reply was businesslike. 'Mr Gilmour isn't in yet—he had an earlier appointment—but he shouldn't be long.'

'He can take as long as he likes.'

The appraising movement of his blue eyes explained why, and Cassie, liking his craggy features and confident manner, knew he was a man she would enjoy going out with.

'How do you like working here?' he went on. 'You're new, aren't you?'

'Yes, she is.' This from Miles, striding into the room. 'You can come in straight away, Clive. I'm ready for you.'

He gave Cassie a cursory nod, then led the man into his office.

He buzzed Cassie half an hour later to bring them coffee, and when she entered with the tray he didn't even raise his head from the advertising layout on his desk. It was difficult to tell if he was genuinely engrossed or angry with her for Saturday night's brush-off.

It was noon before Clive Gordon emerged from his meeting, pausing by her desk to ask if she was attending the party Barlow's were giving that night at the Savoy to launch the publication of a new book by one of their top authors.

'Yes,' she replied.

'Several of us are going on to Annabel's afterwards,' he said, naming London's most exclusive nightclub. 'I hope you're free to come with me?'

Pretty certain Miles would be one of the several, she nodded. 'I'd like that.'

'Great,' Clive Gordon said. 'See you at the Savoy, then.'

As the door closed, Miles buzzed for her to come in. 'Did Clive ask you for a date?' he asked without preamble.

'Why do you want to know?'

'Because he's a notorious womaniser.'

'I'd say that was the pot calling the kettle black!'

'At least I haven't been married and divorced twice,' he grunted.

'Perhaps it will be third time lucky,' she said dulcetly.

His private line rang before he could answer, and as he lifted the receiver Cassie returned to her desk.

Miles didn't mention the subject again, and reverted to the impersonal relationship they had had when she had first come to work for him. Although she had told him this was what she wanted, she was illogically piqued that he could do it so easily. After all, if he found her as disturbing as he had intimated, how could he now stare at her as though she were his maiden aunt?

When Justin called to ask her out she agreed to see him on Friday. It was a sop to her ego to know he fancied her, but she still considered it fairer to him to break off their friendship, and preferred doing it face to face rather than take the coward's way out on the telephone.

Miles left the office early, and, taking advantage of his absence, Cassie went home, mollifying her conscience by reminding herself *she* was the boss and could leave when she liked! She was determined to look her very best tonight, and didn't want to get ready in a rush. The comments Miles had made about Clive didn't deter her from seeing him—rather the opposite, for she had no compunction in using one womaniser to annoy another!

She dressed accordingly. On Saturday she had resisted being too glamorous in case Miles had seen it as a come-on—and a fat lot of good it had done! But tonight she had no such inhibition and pulled out all the stops, choosing a sliver of scarlet silk that clung to her body like a second skin. It left one shoulder bare, and she brushed her hair to one side, curling the waves into chestnut ringlets that cascaded down one side of her creamy neck.

Entering the private room where the party was being held, she was gratified when it took several seconds for her colleagues to recognise her, and she was soon surrounded by a cluster of young men, some of the many who frequented literary receptions.

Remembering she was Miles's secretary, she excused herself and circled the room, enthusing over the new book to any members of the Press who were alone. Clive Gordon arrived late and made an instant bee-line for her. He smelled of newly applied aftershave, and was every inch the top executive as he wandered the room with her, conversing easily with everyone. But then he was in the business of knowing and being known, and she was delighted by his charm and easy manner, aware that it was another irritant for Miles.

In the event she had double the pleasure, for not only did he glower at her when he saw Clive sticking by her side, but he glowered more ferociously when he bumped into her as they entered the nightclub. As she had expected he had a female in tow: a young redhead with a luscious, full-breasted figure, and a doll-like face that was vaguely familiar.

'I hope you enjoy playing with fire?' he muttered to Cassie under his breath.

'After a couple of dates with you I'm used to it.'

'If there's no difference between Clive and myself, why show *me* the door when you're opening it for him?'

'I bet you'd love to know the answer to that!' she whispered with a soft laugh and, turning away, slipped her arm through Clive's.

To her relief he was an interesting companion, being intelligent and witty, with a fund of amusing stories about the many famous people he knew.

'Who's the girl with Miles?' she asked him casually some time later when they were dancing.

'Melody Grace. She had a small part in one of the latest hit musicals.'

'You mean she sings too?'

'Miaow, miaow. She's not bad, actually, but dumb as a bell without a clapper!'

Covertly watching Miles, Cassie was delighted by the boredom on his face. How could he be bothered with bimbos? Or was he only concerned with bed-worthiness? Yet surely sex was better when there was mental communion as well as physical? Her sigh was deep. Obviously it didn't matter to Miles, for all the women he dated were ships that passed in the night, and only Sarah was a permanent port of call.

'Hey, you're not concentrating on me!' Clive's hand tightened on her waist, and, sloughing off all thought of the man she loved, Cassie gave a wide smile and pretended to be having the time of her life.

Soon she was genuinely enjoying herself, for Clive was an excellent dancer.

'It's great having a partner who doesn't trip over my feet,' he said, performing a highly intricate set of steps which she followed perfectly.

'I went to an excellent dancing school in New——' she caught herself in time. 'In Newcastle.'

'Newcastle? You don't have a northern accent.'

'I wasn't there long. We soon moved south.'

'I'm glad. Now I've found you we must do this again.'

The warmth in his voice warned her it would be wiser not to accept. She had nothing to give Clive, and did not wish to use him again as she was using him now.

The music changed to a slower tempo, and Clive gathered her closer. 'This is much better,' he whispered. 'Now I——'

'Mind if I cut in?' Miles said, and before Cassie knew what was happening she found herself whisked away in his arms.

His hands were warm upon her waist, and she forced herself to think of them as any hands, and not the ones which had caressed her so intimately that they had almost tempted her to surrender. She was intensely aware of his body and the heat emanating from it, the feel of the muscles beneath his suit, the firmness of his chest and the hardness of his stomach against hers. He did not talk as he danced, nor in fact did he dance so much as move languidly in time to the music. She knew she should pull away, but could not bring herself to do it. His head lowered, and his cheek rubbed against hers, the faint bristle rasping her skin.

'I didn't know you went in for designer stubble!' she said in an attempt to bring herself down to earth.

'I don't. But I was too pushed for time to shave again before I came out. I hope you don't object?'

Remembering her vow to be all sweetness and light with him, she gave a soft laugh. 'No, I rather like it.'

'In that case I'll do it again.' He rubbed his face slowly along the side of hers, while his hands lightly fondled her bare back, moving up and down her spine.

He wore the musky aftershave she always associated with him, though his hair was devoid of any scent and curled crisply along the back of his neck. She had a strong urge to run her fingers through it, and he uncannily echoed her wish by lifting his hand to touch her shining waves and twine a strand through his fingers.

'Soft as silk,' he murmured.

She snuggled closer, wishing the music would never stop. It didn't, but unfortunately it changed its tempo to an upbeat one, and she raised her head from his shoulder.

'Stay where you are,' he said huskily. 'I like the way we were dancing.'

To prove it he made no concession to the different rhythm of the music, and continued to hold her close, their feet barely moving, their bodies melded one into the other.

'We're wasting so much time, Cassie,' he whispered into her ear. 'I want you so much I can't think straight. Let me take you home tonight.'

Cassie's knees buckled and, had Miles not been holding her tightly, she would have fallen.

'What's wrong?' he asked.

'You. You're the most conceited, thick-skinned swine I've ever met!'

With deep-felt relief she saw they were level with Clive and Melody Grace. 'Time to change partners again,' she said clearly as she twisted free, and Clive instantly swung Melody into Miles's arms and danced Cassie away.

She didn't know how she got through the rest of the evening, so distraught was she because of what Miles had said. So much for her decision to stay in England and fight for him! He wasn't *worth* fighting for. She'd stick to her earlier intention and return to the States. First thing tomorrow she'd hand in her notice and walk out. Then she'd instruct Lionel Newman to draw up an agreement putting Miles in charge of the company. She wouldn't even bother seeing him, wouldn't even tell him her identity. Let him find out for himself when they eventually met, as one day they would.

When Clive saw her home he merely kissed her on the cheek. But then, he was a subtle man, and must have guessed he would be rebuffed if he tried anything more.

'I'll call you in a few days,' he promised, and she nodded, forbearing to say that by then she'd be in America.

Cassie's intention of handing Miles her letter of resignation the instant she walked into the office was prevented by his opening words.

'If you want me to grovel I will.'

'Grovel?' she echoed, raising a delicately curved eyebrow.

'For the gross remark I made last night. My only excuse is that whenever I get close to you I can't think of anything other than—hell! I'll be doing it again if I'm not careful.' He jumped up from behind his desk, and came towards her. 'I'm truly sorry, Cassie. You made your feelings about me quite clear on Saturday, and I had no intention of coming on to you again. But as I said...' Wide shoulders lifted, and he eyed her silently.

Taken aback by his apology—and he acted as if he genuinely meant it—she was not certain what to say. 'That's OK,' she finally managed. 'Just remember to keep your distance!'

His smile was rueful as he went to the door. 'I'll see you this afternoon. I've another meeting with the printers.'

Alone in his office, she took her letter of resignation from her pocket and tore it into shreds. She was crazy to do so, but she couldn't help it any more than she could help her hopes rising again. She tried to tell herself he had apologised because he didn't want to lose her as a secretary, but her heart told her she was beginning to mean something to him, though he was unaware of it. But one day he'd wake up to the fact that he couldn't do without her—and when he did...

Her body trembled, and with a shaky hand she traced the curved back of his chair, wondering how long it would be before she could let her hands touch *him*.

'What on earth went on between you and Mr Gilmour this morning?' Sharon the receptionist asked her over lunch. They usually ate together a couple of times a week at a nearby pasta house.

'Nothing different from usual,' Cassie answered. 'Why?'

'Because I went down with him in the lift as he left for his meeting, and when I said how much everyone here liked you he gave a huge grin and said they'd better not like you enough to touch you, or you'd bite!'

Cassie couldn't restrain a laugh, though her comment was far from truthful. 'I merely mentioned to him that I was extremely ticklish,' she invented, 'and for some reason he found it amusing.'

'What will you do if he puts your statement to the test?'

'That's hardly likely. We work non-stop when he's in the office.'

'It won't be the same when you're together in San Diego,' Sharon teased.

Cassie's mouth dropped open. She had completely forgotten about the international book conference she was supposed to be attending with him there. He had announced his intention of taking her with him a month after she had started working for him.

'It's a great place for making deals, and if I do any I like to have a letter of intent drawn up immediately.'

'Doesn't the hotel provide a secretarial service?' she had asked, for at that time her typing ability had been zero.

'I prefer working with my own secretary,' had come his cool reply. 'When I engaged you I warned you that you'd occasionally have to accompany me abroad.'

'I'd be delighted to,' she had assured him hastily. 'I was merely trying to save you the expense.'

His sarcastic, 'Thanks,' had successfully closed the subject.

'Are you nervous of going away with him?' Sharon's question brought Cassie back to the present.

'No,' she lied. 'I can always put my karate lessons into practice!'

'You'd never catch *me* warding him off,' Sharon sighed. 'I can't imagine any girl resisting him.'

Neither could Cassie, but she was not going to admit it. Returning to her office after her lunch-break, she found Miles leafing through the mid-morning post which she had opened and placed on his desk.

'I see Catherine Barlow's replied to the progress report I sent her,' he commented.

'Yes—I took the liberty of reading it. I hope it's stopped you feeling bitter towards her. She was very complimentary of all you've done.'

Determined to have him eat his words, and perhaps make him feel a grudging respect for 'Catherine', Cassie had spent several hours composing her letter. While not wanting to be too fulsome in her praise of him, she had made no bones about the fact that she was delighted with his stewardship, and had no wish to interfere.

'There's probably some hidden motive behind her praise,' he muttered ungraciously. 'But that isn't what puzzles me. What does is how the letter got here.'

Cassie was mystified. 'Got here? By post, of course.'

'There's a postal strike in New York, and nothing is coming through.'

Wildly she sought for an explanation, and the drone of a low-flying aircraft gave her one. 'It came by air courier. Miss Barlow obviously wanted you to know as soon as possible how pleased she was.'

'I suppose she thinks her opinion is so important to me that I can't wait to hear it!'

Cassie swallowed her annoyance. 'If she'd waited till the strike was over you'd have accused her of not caring. Seems to me she's in a Catch 22 situation as far as you're concerned.'

'I wish you wouldn't keep defending the damn woman!' Miles exclaimed. 'You'll be telling me next I should stop off in New York to see her on my way to San Diego.'

Cassie stared at him, aghast. It was too soon for Miles to discover her identity. She wanted to give him time to fall in love with her.

'If you stopped off in New York you'd have to leave London a day earlier and cancel a dozen appointments,' she said crisply.

'Don't worry. I've better things to do with my time than suck up to a jet-set heiress. Now do me a favour and forget her.'

'Very well.' Cassie paused, then said carefully, 'About San Diego. Am I still going with you?'

'Yes.' He looked directly into her eyes. 'If you're worried about my behaviour, forget it. I've learned my lesson.'

The week leading to their departure passed quickly. She had been dreading telling Justin she no longer wished to see him, but in the event he took it well.

'I hope we can remain friends,' he said. 'You're a great girl, and you'll always be special to me.'

'Thank you, Justin.' Tears blurred her vision and, seeing them, he reached out and clasped her hand.

'It's to my advantage to stay on good terms with all my old girlfriends. Then when they marry and have kids I can become the family paediatrician!'

His joke eased the tension, and she laughed, wishing not for the first time that she could have fallen in love with him.

Depressed at their parting, Cassie accepted another date with Clive for the Saturday. They spent it with friends of his in Surrey, returning late in the evening, when he asked if he could see her the following day.

'I'll be too busy packing.'

'Of course, the conference. I'll call you when you get back.'

He bent to kiss her. His mouth was soft and sensuous, his lips moving gently over hers, though he made no attempt to part them. She tried to respond, but it was impossible, and after a few seconds he let her go.

'Have a good flight, Cassie. And on second thoughts, you call *me* if you want to see me again.'

Clever Clive, she acknowledged as she went to bed. He wasn't going to go where he wasn't welcomed. Trouble was, Miles made all the other men she met seem insipid and dull. What a hopeless situation she was in, and it might continue like this for months.

Perhaps she was contributing to it by her old-fashioned ideas. If she let him make love to her maybe his feelings for her would deepen more quickly. After all, on his own admission he found her interesting and amusing, and this, coming from a man with a low threshold of boredom, must augur well for their future. She sighed. She was indulging in wishful thinking. Miles was still carrying a torch for Sarah, and didn't want involvement with anyone else—that was why he kept changing his girlfriends, for that way he could have sex without commitment whenever the urge took him.

'But not with me,' she said aloud, pounding her pillow with frustration. No matter how much she ached for Miles she would never agree to be one of a number. Not when what she most wanted was to be number one.

CHAPTER FIFTEEN

THE flight to San Diego was direct, which meant leaving from Gatwick. Miles had arranged to call for her at seven-thirty in the morning, and though she was waiting for him, giving him no cause to be in a bad humour, his mood was disgruntled. But then it *had* been for several days, although he had done his best to hide it, and she had sensed an underlying anger that was waiting to surface and erupt.

Despite making it clear he did not wish her to leave, she was beginning to wonder if he was searching for an excuse to fire her. Because of it, she had been so sweet and accommodating that he had found it impossible to fault her. Several times she had caught him watching her with a strange expression, as if trying to fathom the reason behind her sudden passivity.

'Louis Vuitton cases?' he commented as Jack, his chauffeur, placed them in the boot. 'I must be over-paying you.'

Irritated because she had not thought of replacing them, Cassie sought inspiration. 'They're copies from Thailand. You can't tell the difference, can you?'

'So it would seem.'

She stared through the window, praying she wouldn't need to tell any more lies for the next few days. Even trivial ones were starting to trouble her conscience, apart from the difficulty of always having to stay one step ahead of him.

'You've brought an inordinate amount of luggage with you,' he said.

'I know October is officially winter in California, but it can be hot, so I brought a few summer things along.'

'A few! Looks as if you've packed your entire wardrobe.'

'So what? There aren't any luggage restrictions in first class.'

'I suppose that's what you're used to?' he asked sarcastically.

Cassie coloured—not because of his tone, but because of her second silly mistake.

'Of course not,' she denied. 'Other than the flight on Concorde, this is my first time.'

'I've often wondered what you would have done if things hadn't turned out well with Seamus O'Mara,' he remarked. 'Would you still have expected us to pick up the tab for your fare?'

'I acted on impulse and never gave it a thought,' she said truthfully.

'Pity you don't *always* follow your impulses,' he said meaningfully.

He didn't seem to expect a reply, and she didn't make one, and for the remainder of the journey he was silent.

Arriving at Gatwick Airport, Cassie pretended she had to call her mother, and asked Miles to let her have her plane ticket. She'd remain hidden out of sight until he had checked through. That way he wouldn't see she had an American passport! What excuse she would dream up when they landed on the other side of the Atlantic she didn't know, but she was sure she'd think of something!

Miles was already ensconced in the First Class lounge when she entered it, and she wandered over to the book-stall and bought several thick paperbacks, none of which were Barlow's imprint. Returning to her chair, she noticed his raised eyebrows, and too late realised she had spent fifteen pounds. Hardly the amount a genuine secretary would have expended.

'Once I get to an airport I can't resist buying all the latest slush!' she excused.

'I'm glad to see none of ours are included in that statement,' he replied, glancing at the titles.

'I think you *should* have a lighter list. You're losing out on millions of women readers.'

His mouth set in a narrow line, but the announcement of their flight cut short any answer he might have made.

As soon as they were seated on the plane Miles withdrew some papers from his Hermès briefcase and immersed himself in them until dinner was served. Afterwards he dozed, and Cassie noticed how much younger and more vulnerable he looked when relaxed. She had an urge to stroke his smooth skin and kiss the corner of his mouth. But instead she concentrated on the film, a thriller that fortunately held her interest and kept further dangerous thoughts at bay.

After it was over she slept, only waking when Miles lightly shook her shoulder and she saw a steward waiting to serve her with a snack.

They touched down twenty minutes late, but, unlike Los Angeles, Customs formalities were quickly completed. This time it was Miles who didn't go with her through Immigration, explaining he had arranged to call a friend in San Francisco, and might be on the phone for quite a while.

Delighted, Cassie waited in the queue till he was out of sight, then hurriedly went through the sign marked AMERICAN PASSPORT HOLDERS. Lady Luck was certainly smiling on her today. She only hoped it would last!

Quicker than he had said he would, Miles joined her, and within minutes they were driving to the Hotel del Coronado, situated on the Coronado Peninsula, across the bay from San Diego. The journey took fifteen minutes, and was one Cassie was familiar with, having stayed at the hotel on occasions with her parents. Luckily she had not been there for some time, and, knowing how hotel staff moved around, she hoped no one would recognise her.

There was no need to pretend an interest in the scenery. However many times she saw the bay, she never tired of its natural beauty. The Pacific ocean was sparkling blue cobalt beneath a cloudless sky, the air still warm and balmy as the late afternoon sun began to sink on the horizon. In spite of Miles's warning it was difficult not to feel in a holiday mood as they crossed the bridge spanning the causeway, and came to a halt outside the main entrance to the hotel.

'The Dell', as it was affectionately known, was of Victorian architecture at its very best, and no expense had been spared on its construction in the late nineteenth century. The white-painted building, with its red-tiled roof, sandcastle turrets, superb garden setting and stately trees, epitomised the grand manner, and had become a living legend, with visits by nearly every one of the nation's presidents, as well as thousands of celebrities from all over the world.

The vast entrance hall, with its dark oak panelling, red and gold carpet, and magnificent central glass chandelier, was crowded with fellow conventioneers and their companions. But, with usual American efficiency, they were not kept waiting for long.

Cassie's relief that no member of the staff recognised her was short-lived, for as she bent down to register she heard the voice of the manager.

'Nice to see you again, Miss Elliot,' he enthused. 'You've been away far too long.'

'Thank you, Peter. It's nice to be back.'

'I didn't notice your name on the guest list, or I'd——'

'I'm part of the convention,' she cut in. 'And this is Miles Gilmour, my employer.' She threw the manager a pleading glance, and he seemed to understand something was amiss. Smoothly he went on his way, but his warm welcome had aroused Miles's curiosity.

'You certainly get around,' he stated as they headed for the lift.

'I worked here,' she lied, hating herself for yet another deception, yet knowing it might look odd if she admitted to staying here. 'During my trip around the world I worked in several hotels,' she elaborated. At least that covered her in case they spent a night in Los Angeles, and the same thing happened.

'But why did the manager call you Miss Elliot, and not Cassie?' Miles was evidently not satisfied with her reply.

'He's a stickler for formality,' she said. 'If he had his way all the staff would still be wearing Victorian dress!'

'What was your job here?'

'I did several things.' She was deliberately vague. 'I'll show you around later if you like?'

'I would.' For the first time that day he smiled at her. 'Settle yourself in, and I'll meet you in the lobby in an hour. Is that enough time?'

'Yes—in spite of having my whole wardrobe to unpack!' she replied saucily.

He chuckled. 'Welcome back, Miss Elliot. I was getting heartily bored with Miss Sweetness and Light!'

They were both on the same floor, but their rooms were the length of a corridor apart, and she wondered if this had been deliberate on Miles's part. Now that friendly relations had been restored she would have the courage to ask him.

The décor was in shades of blue, white and grey, and her terrace overlooked the fine-sand beach and the ocean beyond. The adjoining bathroom was equipped with equal luxury, and as soon as she unpacked she had a shower to revive her flagging spirits.

When she returned to the bedroom a bottle of champagne in an ice-bucket stood on the central table, with a handwritten card from the manager welcoming her again. There was also a large bowl of fruit and an exquisite arrangement of flowers. Thank goodness she was meeting Miles downstairs. It would have been hard explaining all this away!

He was talking to another man when she joined him. Like Miles and herself he was wearing a convention badge printed with his name and company. He was German, but his English was almost flawless.

'I was just telling Miles I came here on my honeymoon fifteen years ago, and have not been back since. But the hotel is exactly as I remembered it, which is a plus in its favour. One gets tired of customised hotels, however luxurious.'

As soon as he decently could Miles extricated them from the garrulous Berliner, and turned his attention to Cassie.

'Your room all right?' he enquired.

'It's sensational. But then "the Dell" is one of the best hotels in the States.'

'You didn't work in its publicity department by any chance?' he teased.

She smiled and shook her head, then guided him round the hotel. He listened with interest as she told him that when it was built it was the largest structure, outside of New York, to have electric lighting.

'Thomas Eddison personally supervised the work, and pulled the switch on the hotel's first electrically lit Christmas tree,' she added.

'Ever considered writing a book about this place?' Miles asked.

'I might do if you gave me a big enough advance!'

'Enough to buy genuine Vuitton luggage?'

'How did you guess?' she said gaily, and led him to the bar.

'This might be our last free time alone for a while,' he said as they settled themselves behind a corner table in the heavily carved oak room. 'There's a pre-dinner reception at eight, and the schedule for the next couple of days is pretty heavy.' A waiter approached them, and Miles asked what she wanted to drink.

'They do an excellent Californian champagne here,' she said.

'Two, please,' he ordered, then settled back against the green upholstered chair. 'You look fresh as a daisy, though I'm sure you're tired.'

'I'm not too bad at the moment. What about you?'

'I travel so much I know how to cope with jet lag. I avoid alcohol when I'm in flight, and take specific vitamins.'

'I noticed you popping pills.'

'I hope you didn't think I was an addict!'

'It never crossed my mind.'

Their eyes met and held, and even in the subdued lighting she discerned silver flecks in the deep grey irises.

'I feel very relaxed,' he remarked, sipping his champagne. 'You're soothing on the nerves, Cassie. Unlike many women you know when to keep quiet.'

'Most men dislike idle chatter,' she shrugged, pleased by the compliment.

'If by that you mean gossip, then I agree.'

'Men gossip as much as women,' she protested. 'And we find cars and sports as boring as you do hairdressers and clothes.'

'We also talk about our conquests.'

'So do we. Though I think women are more honest and are ready to admit to failures.'

He popped some peanuts into his mouth, and chewed them thoughtfully. 'Have you had many affairs?' he asked.

'Why are you interested?' she parried.

'Because it would explain your lack of interest in me. Perhaps you've had a bad experience, and are frightened of being let down again.'

'I want a stable relationship,' she informed him. 'I thought you understood that.'

'By stable I assume you mean marriage?'

'That would be the ultimate aim. I want children, and they'll have enough problems to contend with without the label of illegitimacy.'

'That's hardly considered a drawback these days,' he protested. 'I believe forty per cent of mothers in the UK are unmarried.'

'But how many from choice? Statistics never tell the whole story.'

'I do believe you're an old-fashioned girl at heart!'

'I never said I wasn't. You don't know me as well as you think you do, Miles.'

'It's not for want of trying.'

Cassie refused to be drawn, and Miles peered at her across the table. 'I do believe you're blushing!'

'No, I'm not. The reflection from the pink shades gives that impression.'

'I've noticed you blushing before when the subject of sex cropped up,' he went on, ignoring her denial. 'It's attractive and unusual—unusual enough to make me wonder if you're a virgin.'

This time she did blush, and he chuckled. 'Well, well, wonders never cease. You aren't unusual, Cassie, you're unique!'

It was useless of her to argue, and she was furious for giving herself away. Now he would think the only reason she hadn't gone to bed with him was because she was saving herself for marriage, when in truth she was holding out for love.

'When you say "unique",' she responded drily, 'don't you mean antique?'

He chuckled again. 'Not in the sense of being an old relic, but as a collector's item you'd certainly be something to treasure.'

'Well said.' Her tone was drier. 'You should have been a writer, not a publisher.'

'Don't mock me, Cassie. I meant it as a compliment.'

'So did I, Miles.'

The status quo restored, they smiled at one another.

'Fancy another drink?' he asked.

'It's getting late. I'd better go and change for dinner.'

He signed the bill, and sauntered to the lift.

'I'll meet you in the lobby at eight,' he said as they reached their floor. 'Then we can go into the reception together.'

Cassie had already resolved what to wear. Simple in the extreme, though not in price, for it was a Bill Blass, the soft green silk jersey covered her slender figure, while the subtle draping enhanced every curve. She applied

less make-up than usual, feeling the intricate cut of her
dress was statement enough, and only used mascara to
thicken the lashes that framed her sherry-brown eyes,
and a translucent lipstick that drew attention to the soft
contours of her mouth. There was no time to fuss with
her hair, and she swept it up into a loose chignon, held
in place with a diamanté comb, allowing a few chestnut
fronds to escape at the sides and nape of her neck, thus
drawing attention to the graceful curve.

Miles stared at her admiringly as she emerged from
the lift, and she returned the compliment. His dark blue
suit was impeccably cut, and drew attention to his wide
shoulders, while his white shirt emphasised the raven
gleam of his hair.

'You're stunning,' he said as he came towards her. 'Is
your dress new?'

'Yes. I've been saving it for an occasion.'

'I'm glad you thought being with me warranted it.'

Taking her arm, he steered her towards the private
suite where the reception and dinner was being held. Her
spine tingled at the touch of his hand, but she refused
to let herself be affected by his proximity, determined
not to succumb to any easy gesture on his part.

The room was filling rapidly, and the scent of expensive cigars and perfume permeated the air. Miles
stopped several times to speak to acquaintances as they
made their way to the bar at the far end. The men stared
admiringly at Cassie, while the women could barely
conceal their envy. She was certain they knew of Miles's
reputation with women, and doubted that they accepted
she was his secretary; they probably assumed it was a
polite euphemism for girlfriend.

'You're certainly a contrast to Mrs Darcy,' Miles
smiled, when she voiced the thought aloud. 'But if you're
worried about your reputation I'm sure they'll be convinced when they see you taking notes.'

'I suppose all the wives and girlfriends will be sunning
themselves.'

'Don't worry. You'll have enough time off to acquire a tan to show your friends.'

Next day he was as good as his word, working her until lunchtime, and then giving her the whole afternoon to herself. On the second day, after his address to the conference, which was very well received, he unexpectedly joined her at the pool. Had he not stopped directly in front of her, but walked by, she might not have recognised him, for in his jazzily patterned swimming trunks he looked entirely different. Yet the broad shoulders and chest, the narrow hips and strong, sinewy legs exuded the same dynamic forcefulness as his character.

He surveyed her brief bikini in silence, and Cassie was glad her sunglasses gave her a protective covering.

'You're full of surprises,' he said at last. 'I expected to find you in a chemise!'

'With or without a mob-cap!'

He laughed. 'Knowing how you prefer to play safe, you probably have a chastity belt beneath your bikini bottom!'

'And the only key, other than mine, is kept in a Swiss bank vault!'

White teeth flashed as he grinned. 'Fancy joining me for a swim? Unless you're worried the lock will rust!'

She jumped up, and without a word dived into the pool. He was hard on her heels, striking out with strong strokes, and reaching the far end long before she did, after which he turned and swam towards her.

'So there *is* something I do better than you,' he mocked.

'I wasn't trying to beat you,' she said indignantly. 'Give me——'

Her words were lost as he dunked her below the surface, and then reached out and heaved her up beside him. Laughing and spluttering, she put her hands on his shoulders and allowed him to tow her towards the side.

'Now if you really think you can beat me...' he enquired humorously.

With a shake of her head she accepted the challenge, but, though she was fast, he was faster, and he touched the blue-tiled wall first. He hauled himself up to sit on the side, then offered her a helping hand. She shook the water from her hair, and tried to stifle her breathlessness.

'I accept defeat gracefully. And as the loser always buys the drinks, what would you like?' she asked.

'Nothing alcoholic,' he answered. 'I had too much wine at lunch.'

He sat down on the sunbed and stretched out full length, squinting up at her in the sunlight as she gave an order for two freshly squeezed orange juices to a passing waiter.

'Just the job,' he commented lazily.

Cassie lay down beside him, and they chatted inconsequentially until their drinks arrived. Afterwards they lay silently sun-worshipping, the heat radiating through their bodies and evaporating the dampness of their costumes.

Turning her head to speak to him, she saw he had fallen asleep with the suddenness of a small child. In her mind's eye she pictured him as a little boy, with unruly dark hair and a thin but sturdy frame. No doubt he had been obstinate and strong-minded even then, yet thoughtful and honest, too. No wonder he had been spoiled by his three sisters and mother. And the women in his life had gone on spoiling him ever since. With a little sigh she closed her eyes and drifted off to sleep.

She awakened with the sensation of being watched, and turning her head found Miles resting on one elbow and staring down at her.

'Had a good sleep?' he questioned.

'Mmm. And you?'

'I just had my eyes closed.'

Cassie stretched, and turned over on to her stomach. 'Do you usually snore when you're awake?'

'I've never snored in my life,' he said indignantly.

'You mean no one's ever had the courage to tell you!'

'Was I really?'

'No. I was teasing.'

Their eyes met and held, and though her gaze faltered under the intensity of his, she had no desire to turn away. She longed to be close to him, and the wish to be held in his arms again and feel his lips on hers was so strong it was almost overwhelming.

He seemed able to read her thoughts, and a pulse throbbed at his temple. 'Cassie, I——'

'Hello, you two. We've been searching everywhere for you.'

With a muttered imprecation Miles swung away from her, and Cassie saw the German publisher and his wife regarding them.

'There are no meetings tomorrow,' the German said, 'and my wife and I are going to Sea World for the day. We wondered if you'd care to join us?'

'I'm afraid I can't,' Miles replied. 'I'm going to Los Angeles on business. But perhaps Cassie would like to go?' He glanced at her enquiringly.

'I've already been several times,' she excused herself. 'I think I'd rather stay by the pool.'

'You can come with me to Los Angeles,' Miles offered when the couple were out of earshot. 'But I'll be tied up all day, and you'll have to amuse yourself.'

She hesitated. Her closest friend had married and moved to Beverly Hills six months ago, and it would be marvellous to see her again. Yet on the debit side it meant spending several hours in a car with Miles.

'I should be free by six, and we can dine at Le Bistro,' he said, breaking the silence. 'It's one of the best restaurants in LA, and I guarantee you'll see quite a few stars.'

Cassie Elliot, stepdaughter of Luther, couldn't have cared less, but the Cassie who was Miles's secretary looked suitably impressed.

'If you can promise me a sighting of Tom Cruise...'

'If he isn't there I'll get you his picture!'

'Autographed?'

'If need be I'll sign it myself!'

'Done! I'm looking forward to that dinner.'

A dark eyebrow lifted. 'It will be nice if we can behave like two friends who enjoy each other's company, instead of sparring like cat and dog.'

Danger signals flashed before Cassie's eyes, but she ignored them and threw caution to the wind. Hadn't she proved that in spite of her feelings for him she was able to resist temptation?

'I agree with you,' she said. 'But remember this is a truce, not an outright victory!'

CHAPTER SIXTEEN

At seven the next morning Cassie was waiting for Miles at the front entrance of the hotel, casual in a cream silk shirtwaister, her luxuriant hair tied back from her face with a matching bandeau. The simple style drew attention to her high cheekbones and full mouth, without in any way detracting from her businesslike appearance.

Yet her emotional response when she saw Miles coming towards her was far from businesslike, for he was absurdly attractive in lightweight stone suit over white shirt, tan and white tie, and tan Gucci loafers.

'Just as I anticipated,' he greeted her. 'On time, and perfectly dressed for the occasion!'

'And good morning to you, too!' she smiled happily, her bones telling her that this was going to be a wonderful day.

The drive to Los Angeles took over two hours, and they made desultory conversation. But the atmosphere between them was relaxed and, seated comfortably in the back of the air-conditioned Cadillac, the outside temperature of eighty degrees presented no problems.

'It's going to be a real scorcher,' Miles commented as he dropped her outside the Beverly Wiltshire Hotel, and arranged to meet her in the hotel bar for a pre-dinner drink. 'Have you decided how you're going to spend the day?'

'I might get a cab to the Getty Museum,' she replied. 'Or mooch up and down Rodeo Drive.'

He took out his wallet and extracted two hundred dollars. 'For you,' he said, pressing them into her hand. 'So that you don't just have to window-shop. A travel allowance,' he added as she went to protest.

She still wanted to refuse, but decided it was churlish to do so. Not that she had any intention of spending the money on herself. But spend it she would, and buy something for Miles.

Familiar with the stores, she went straight to Tiffany's and purchased a slim crocodile notebook with an equally slim gold pen hidden inside. It cost three times the amount he had given her, but she doubted he would be *au fait* with the price.

Then she hailed a cab and headed for Bel Air, where her friend Gail lived in a pink-shuttered white mansion that resembled a wedding-cake.

'I've been counting the hours till you got here,' Gail greeted her, hugging her close. 'I couldn't believe my ears when you called me last night. I'd have murdered you if you'd come to San Diego without seeing me!'

'I'm not a free agent, you know.'

'How *is* the ogre, by the way?'

'Breathing fire without the brimstone!'

'So you've tamed him!'

Cassie laughed. 'Hardly.'

'Tell me your latest news,' Gail ordered, leading her across a marble hall to a terrace overlooking an Olympic-size pool.

Settling into a padded lounger, Cassie did, finding great relief in confessing her true feelings for Miles, which she hadn't done with her mother or stepfather.

'I'm glad you no longer see yourself as a publishing tycoon,' Gail said as the saga came to an end. 'It's tough being at the helm of a big company, and for the next few years I think you should concentrate on getting married and having a family.'

'With the right man I'd be delighted to, but——'

'You can't waste your life pining over this Miles. Personally, I think he enjoys playing the field, and I don't for a second believe he's still in love with this Sarah woman. If he is, and he's still jumping into other beds, then he's best forgotten. I think you should tell him who you are, and hare back home.'

'You make it sound so easy,' Cassie said miserably. 'I suppose I'm hoping he'll see the light and fall in love with me. Sometimes I think he already has, but won't admit it to himself.'

'Even if what you say is true, then he's in love with Cassie Elliot, not Catherine Barlow. And will he be able to separate the two? You played a heck of a trick on him, and he might not forgive you for it.'

'Hey, you're supposed to be making me feel better, not worse!'

Gail tossed her long blonde hair. 'I'm your best friend, honey, and I say it as I see it. Come clean with him sooner rather than later.'

When Cassie entered the Beverly Wiltshire bar, brim-full of all the latest movie gossip, Miles was already waiting for her, and a warm smile lit up his face as he rose to greet her.

'You look as if you've had a good time,' he observed, and unexpectedly bent and kissed her cheek. 'I bet that means you've been shopping all day!'

'Right!'

'Then you'll be in need of a drink.' He moved aside, and she saw a bottle of champagne—not Californian this time, but Roederer Crystal—cooling in an ice-bucket on their table.

'Your meeting must have been highly successful,' she said as she sat down and accepted a brimming glass from him.

'It was. But if it hadn't been I'd have ordered two bottles!'

'I approve of that philosophy.'

'I shouldn't think you've ever needed drink to cheer you up.'

'I was just going to say the same of you!'

An odd expression crossed his face. 'I've had my blue moments.'

Sarah, she thought, and her pleasurable mood evaporated.

'For a girl who was shopping all day,' he went on, changing the subject, 'you're remarkably free of parcels.'

'That's easy to explain.' Opening her purse, she took out the notebook, wrapped in Tiffany paper. 'This is for you, Miles. My mother taught me good girls never accept money from any man other than their husband,' she said solemnly as she handed it to him. 'And, as you know, I'm a *very* good girl!'

'I do indeed.' He undid the package. 'It's beautiful,' he murmured with genuine pleasure. 'But it looks far more expensive than the two hundred dollars I gave you.'

'It was on sale,' she explained hurriedly. 'A real bargain.'

'I still wish you'd bought something for yourself instead.'

She shook her head. 'There's nothing I need.'

'Oh, come on, I'm sure you can think of something. What if you won a lottery—a million dollars, say?'

Here was her chance to confess who she was, yet she couldn't bring herself to do it—not here in this noisy bar, with people coming and going. And not while they were at the conference, either. Much better to wait until they had returned to England, when she could present him with the contract making him a partner. Surely that would sweeten the sourness he would feel when he learned her identity?

'Come on,' Miles repeated. 'What would you do with a million dollars? Buy an apartment, a Mercedes, jewellery?'

With an effort Cassie entered into the game he was playing. 'A restaurant,' she stated, straight-faced.

'A what?'

'You said I was a good enough cook to open my own.'

'So I did. I'd forgotten.'

'Oh.' She made herself look disappointed, and he rose to the bait.

'When I'm with you,' he said deeply, 'food is the last thing on my mind.'

She was considering a reply when he dropped some money on the table and suggested they leave.

As he had promised, they dined at Le Bistro, where they were seated at one of the best tables. Miles had to be well-known there to warrant such treatment, and well liked, too, for the staff greeted him as a friend rather than a customer. It was easy to see why. In spite of an air that marked him as someone who was used to being in command, he displayed no condescension or arrogance towards the people serving them.

'You said your day was successful,' Cassie remarked as they savoured their first course of lobster soufflé. 'Does that mean West Coast sales are good?'

'Among other things.'

'What sort of other things? Or don't you want to talk about them?'

'They're not all that interesting.'

'I find everything you do interesting,' she ventured, emboldened by too much champagne. 'But you've guessed that already, haven't you?'

'In spite of your denials—yes!' he responded humorously. 'And I have to admit you've made me rethink my ideas on relationships.'

'Really?' Purposefully she kept her voice non-committal.

'Yes,' he confessed with a hint of embarrassment. 'You've proved the exception to my rule.' Setting down his fork, he reached across the table for her hand. 'I realise you aren't the sort of girl who'd give herself to a man unless she loved him, and I——' He paused, then went on abruptly, 'I don't want a casual affair with you, Cassie. If I hadn't been so damned obstinate I'd have admitted it sooner. But I've been running free for so long I didn't relish the thought of a harness!'

It took superhuman determination for Cassie to restrain the hope burgeoning inside her. But she was so scared of misunderstanding him and making an idiot of herself that she remained silent.

'For God's sake say something!' he burst out.

'I—I'm not sure what you expect me to say.'

'Yes.'

'Yes?'

A fine sheen of sweat marked his brow. 'I'm proposing to you, Cassie.'

Relinquishing her hand, he leaned back in his chair. A lock of hair had fallen forward on his brow, and he raked it back impatiently. His face was set in taut lines, and he gave every appearance of a man on the rack.

Cassie clasped her shaking hands in her lap. Never in her wildest dreams had she anticipated a proposal of marriage tonight, and she couldn't help wondering what had precipitated it. Yet why not simply accept the joy of knowing he was in love with her and wanted her to be his wife? And how deeply he *must* love her for it to have changed his whole way of thinking. The full awareness of what this meant swept over her, for his love would hardly turn to hate when she confessed to being Catherine Barlow. But she wouldn't tell him now. She wanted nothing to mar this wonderful moment.

'I—I can't believe it,' she stammered. 'You've taken me by surprise.'

'I've surprised myself, too!' he admitted. 'But how about yes, for a change?'

'You didn't expect any other answer, did you?' she said happily. 'Yes, Miles. Yes, yes, yes!'

'Darling!' he murmured huskily, and reached for her hand again. 'What a stupid place for me to propose. I can't even kiss you!'

'I know. I hope your timing won't always be so bad?'

'I can guarantee that!'

Warm colour stole into her cheeks and she hastily resumed eating, though the soufflé might well have been cardboard for all her awareness of it.

'When did you know you loved me?' Cassie asked a little while later as she pushed her main course round her plate. It was a delicious seafood platter, but she was too full of happiness to have room for food.

'I've fancied you like mad since the moment I saw you, but it wasn't until we were on the plane coming over here, and I fell asleep and then woke up to see you sleeping beside me, that I knew I always wanted you to be there when I woke up.'

It was the nicest thing Miles had ever said to her, and her eyes shimmered with tears.

'Let's get out of here,' he said thickly, 'before I do something that will land us on the front page of the *Los Angeles Times*!'

She nodded, and he dropped a fistful of dollars on the table, murmured a few words to their bemused waiter, and hurried her from the restaurant.

Their chauffeur-driven car was waiting for them, and the instant they were in the back, with the glass partition closed between themselves and the driver, Miles drew her into his arms.

His kiss was deep and searching, demanding an intimacy she had no hesitation in allowing him. She loved this man more than life itself. Indeed, without him she had no life. Her lips parted, giving him access to the sweet moisture within, and he groaned deep in his throat as his tongue skilfully slid against hers. There was a fluttering deep inside her, and she pressed closer to him, resenting the clothes that separated them.

His hand cupped her breast, his fingers inserting themselves into the open V of her dress to caress the swelling curve. The fluttering became a tremor, the tremor a spasm, and there was a burning ache between her thighs. She gasped and clutched at him, and with a strangled sound he lifted his mouth from hers.

'Darling, no, not here,' he rasped, and drew away from her. But his hand gripped hers and held it against his side so that she felt the tremble of his body. 'Why the hell did I have a chauffeur drive us today?' he muttered. 'If I'd been driving myself we——'

'Would have ended up in the back seat like a couple of overheated teenagers!' she finished for him.

His mouth quirked. 'Don't knock it. Right now I could emulate them!'

'Me too,' she confessed.

His head lowered to hers. 'Does that mean you wouldn't say "no" a third time?'

'No—I mean yes. Oh, that's wrong too. It's no, isn't it?'

'I'm not sure,' he said whimsically, and she half raised herself, and touched the tip of her tongue to his ear.

'Is that answer enough?' she whispered.

'Absolutely.'

During the rest of the long drive back to the hotel they sat close together, an intimacy established that had no need for words. And, indeed, Miles was silent for most of the journey, as if respecting the emotions she must be experiencing, and giving her time for reflection.

'Are you sure?' he asked huskily, as they reached their floor in the hotel, and stepped out of the lift.

'I was never more certain of anything,' she replied and, twining her arm through his, led him to her room.

As soon as she switched on the light Cassie realised her mistake, for she had forgotten about the champagne, flowers and fruit from the manager. And of course Miles remarked on it at once.

'Who sent you all this? A secret admirer?'

She shook her head, thinking fast. 'The manager. When I rang him to see why, I found they were meant for a honeymoon couple on the floor below. But he insisted I keep everything.'

'Very generous,' Miles said expressionlessly.

'Shall I put the champagne on ice? Then we can have it later,' she suggested quickly.

'Later all we'll want to do is sleep,' he said, pulling her close. There was no hesitation now, no questioning. He wanted her, and was master of the situation.

With practised ease he moved both hands beneath her knees and swung her off her feet, carrying her across the room to the king-size bed, and placing her gently upon it. His breath quickened, and his grey eyes grew slumberous as he stared down at her. Then he reached for the bedside-lamp, and switched it on before turning off the centre one.

Swiftly he undid his shirt, the buckle of his belt, the zip of his trousers, and then he was naked. Even though Cassie had frequently seen her brothers in various stages of undress, she had expected to feel some embarrassment with Miles. Yet she didn't. It was as if they had been lovers for ever, and when, with the skill of experience, he reached for the zip of her dress and swiftly pulled it down over the curve of her hips to expose her near-naked body beneath, it felt completely natural.

Lacy briefs removed the last obstacle, and then it was flesh upon flesh, warm and sensual. With a low cry he rained kisses on her mouth, then his lips travelled down her throat until they reached the hollow of her breasts. Turning his head, his tongue caressed a tight pink nub. It hardened at his touch and rose high, as did the pulsing muscle between his legs, and with a groan he drew the nipple into his mouth and sucked it.

'Beautiful,' he murmured, 'so beautiful,' and shifted away to look into her face and then down the length of her body. 'God, how I want you!'

Taking her hand, he guided it between his legs to show her. With instinctive skill she ran her fingers lightly up and down the throbbing length, teasing and rubbing until he cried out and pushed her hand away.

'No more, sweetheart,' he whispered, trailing kisses along the soft swell of her stomach to the wet, engorged inner sanctum, where his tongue aroused incredible sensations as he licked, sucked and nibbled.

She writhed in an agony of passion, and tried to pull him over her. 'I want you,' she cried. 'I want you.'

'Not yet.' He raised his head from her, allowing the peak to subside, though keeping her passion alive with his hands.

'Hold me,' he said thickly, his breath hot against her ear.

Lovingly she complied, as aroused by giving pleasure as she was by receiving it. Greatly daring, she emulated him, and with lips and hands she encompassed his manhood, excited to feel the velvet hardness enlarge even more. But he still did not lose control, knowing when to soothe her, knowing not to over-excite. Only when she was sobbing for him, begging him to enter her, did he straddle her and part her thighs. But even then he denied her, the heated rod rubbing along the damp curls between her legs, the tip slightly pressing inwards and then withdrawing until she reared up and caught hold of it.

'*Now,*' he groaned, and thrust forward so fast and smoothly that her pain was only momentary, and with an echoing cry the soft folds of her encompassed him and absorbed him completely.

To her surprise he went motionless, and when she lifted her lids to stare into his eyes she found the grey depths dark with passion.

'Easy, darling,' he whispered, his hands coming behind her to cup her buttocks and lift them tighter against him.

There was a movement inside her like the flutter of a bird, and involuntarily she responded to it with a movement of her own. His indrawn breath was loud in her ear, and with a gasp he pressed her back upon the bed and came hard down on her, beginning the age-old rhythm. Cassie was lost in sensation, conscious only of the hardness reaching up into her, arousing her to new heights, new peaks of desire that had her clawing at him in a frenzy that equalled his, until with a great shout his entire body convulsed and his life-force flooded into her, its heat sending her into a shuddering orgasm, so that they climaxed together, soared into a blinding high of passion and then slowly drifted down into bliss.

Neither of them moved, and for what seemed aeons they lay together, bodies warm and moist, legs inter-twined and eyes closed, languorously drowsy with the exertion.

Nestling against his chest, the softness of his hair beneath her cheek, Cassie was swamped by a satisfaction she had never thought possible. Not merely the satisfaction of passion enjoyed and spent, but of a fulfilment that came from love. Savouring the thought, she knew it had been worth waiting for; to have given in to desire might have appeased frustration, but would never have resulted in such a joyous coupling.

'I'm sorry I was inexperienced,' she said softly. 'But I promise you I'm a quick learner!'

'You already know plenty.'

She sighed contentedly. 'I hope you don't believe in long engagements, Miles. I know we've started the honeymoon before the wedding, but——'

'I don't believe in engagements at all,' he cut her short. 'Particularly ours.'

'You mean you want to get married straight away?'

'I mean I'm not going to marry you,' he said carefully.

Cassie sat up, not certain she had heard him correctly. But one glance at his face assured her she had. It could have been cast in bronze, so hard and inanimate it was. 'I—er—I don't understand,' she stumbled.

He propped himself up on one elbow and regarded her. 'Perhaps if I call you Catherine, you will.'

Fear seared through her like a flame, and she steeled herself to keep it from showing. 'How did you find out? And when?'

'Today,' he answered, and swung away from her off the bed. In nude perfection he strode across to the chair where he had flung his clothes in passionate haste the night before, and with equal haste—though with the icy passion of fury—he flung them on. 'My meeting in Los Angeles was to consider whether to buy a small chain of bookstores that suddenly came up for sale on the West Coast. I decided to go for it, but I needed Miss Barlow's approval and rang her apartment in New York. A manservant informed me she was in London, and when I asked if he had her phone number there—surprise, surprise, he gave me yours.'

Cassie was furious with herself. What an idiot she was not to have thought of something like this occurring. But there was no point in regret. What was done was done, and in the past. It was the future—hers and Miles's—that concerned her now. Always supposing they still had a future.

'I had already made up my mind to tell you the truth,' she said, unable to control the shakiness of her voice. 'But I was waiting for the right moment.'

'And when was that going to be?' he questioned harshly. 'When you were ready to throw me out and run the company yourself? That *was* your plan, wasn't it?'

'Only at the very beginning,' she admitted. 'And only because I inadvertently overheard you telling Lionel Newman you'd walk out the minute I stepped over the threshold. Once I got to know you I realised no one could run Barlow's as well as you, and I decided to put you in complete charge.'

'Is that so?' His sarcasm was heavy. 'I assume you had a reason for not telling me, or were you having too much fun carrying on with your charade?'

'It was no fun, and I had the very best reason.' Her voice was urgent. She had to appease his anger, make him understand why she had remained silent. If she failed, he would walk away from her. 'I was waiting for Lionel to complete all the legal formalities. I wanted to give you the new agreement at the same time that I told you who I was.'

'And for light relief meanwhile, you amused yourself by pretending to fall for me.'

'It wasn't pretending,' she cried. 'I——'

'Don't give me that! You're nothing but a scheming bitch! You were bored with your life and thought you'd relieve the boredom with a new game called Barlow's. Making me fall for you added spice to the game.'

'You're wrong! It was the last thing I wanted. That's why I kept my distance. But I loved you in spite of myself. That's another reason why I didn't confess who

I was earlier. I was hoping—waiting—for you to feel the same way about me.'

'What sort of love can you build on deception?' he ground out. 'God! All that talk of relationships... You make me sick!'

'I wanted to tell you the truth,' she reiterated, 'but I was scared you'd walk out.'

'And you were right. Because that's what I'm going to do now!' He picked up his jacket and went to the door.

'Miles!' she cried, and, pulling the sheet around her, jumped out of bed and ran towards him. 'Miles, don't go! We've got to talk!'

'No.' He fended her off with hard hands. 'The talking's over. I'm finished with you and I'm finished with Barlow's. Find another fool for a partner. With your delectable body as a perk you won't have too much difficulty.'

Pain seared her, but knowing that he was hurt too, Cassie forgave him. 'I love you, Miles. Please believe that. I'm sorry for what I did, but can't you understand why I——?'

'No, I can't,' he cut in, all anger gone, his tone weary. 'You're like a small child, Cassie. You think that saying sorry will put things right. But it won't. I've met some scheming, selfish women in my time, but you're in a class by yourself!' Unexpectedly his hand shot out and gripped her chin, tilting her face up to his. 'How does it feel to be outclassed, Cassie? To know I finally saw through your Miss Innocent act, your "waiting for true love" scenario, and played you at your own game?'

The blood drained from Cassie's head, and she felt she was going to faint. 'That—that part wasn't a game,' she said faintly.

'Well, it was for me!' His grip on her chin tightened. 'How does it feel to be on the receiving end?' His lips curved back in a travesty of a smile. 'Last night was the only thing worth remembering about you. Whatever else you are, Miss Barlow, you're great in bed—assuming that wasn't an act, too?'

Brutally he flung her aside, and she staggered against the wall. Pain shot through her side, but it was nothing to the pain that squeezed her heart. 'Get out!' she said dully. 'Get out of my life.'

'Delighted to oblige.' He actually smiled at her. 'Breaking my service contract will cost you plenty, but then you have plenty, Miss Elliot, so why should you care?'

He opened the door, but as he crossed the threshold he stopped, turned back, and pressed the black crocodile notebook she had given him into her hand.

'Keep this.' His voice was dry as tissue paper. '*My* mother told me never to accept presents from strange women, and they don't come any stranger than you!'

With that he was gone, striding away from her into a future in which she would play no part.

CHAPTER SEVENTEEN

WEEKS later Cassie had not recovered from the dreadful half-hour that had destroyed her dream of a future as Miles's wife. It had a nightmare quality about it, but unlike most nightmares there was no waking up from it.

Never had she imagined he would be completely unforgiving and lacking in understanding. She had expected anger, yes, but had thought he would soon see the humorous side to her pretence, particularly when he realised it was his intolerant attitude towards the then unknown Catherine Barlow that had prompted her to embark on it.

Within two hours of their dreadful scene in her bedroom she was winging her way to New York to see her parents and put them in the picture. Not the total picture—self-preservation stopped her from admitting how cunningly he had seduced her—but enough for them to know that Miles was no longer running Barlow Publishing, and that she was remaining in England to do so for the foreseeable future.

Then it was on to London and a painful meeting with Lionel Newman who, though too kind to say 'I told you so', was too honest to offer her false comfort.

'In my opinion Miles will never return to Barlow's no matter what inducement you offer him.'

'I still want you to send him the agreement you've drawn up,' she insisted. 'You can also tell him he can buy out my entire shareholding.'

'You can't mean that!' The lawyer was shocked. 'Your late father would——'

'My late father had no use for me during his lifetime, and the legacy he left me has brought me only pain,' she

159

confessed. 'I mean it, Lionel. If Miles wants to buy me out, he can.'

In the event, Miles had refused to have anything further to do with Barlow's, sending Lionel a curt letter saying there was nothing further to discuss.

Cassie wasn't surprised. A man who could behave as he had done in San Diego was unlikely to have any forgiveness in his soul. Even when she looked at her deceit in the worst possible light, she still considered his way of paying her back to be unbelievably cruel. To have pretended to love her, to have proposed marriage in order to get her into bed showed a ruthlessness that filled her with horror.

Yet though she told herself all these things Cassie could not stop loving him. For a while, each time the telephone rang she would momentarily hope it was Miles. But despite agreeing to an extremely generous golden handshake, there was no word from him, and he clearly accepted it as his due. The only news she had of him was gleaned from the financial pages of the newspapers. He had set up his own publishing company, financed by David Hollister's merchant bank, and several authors—including Seamus O'Mara—as well as some editorial staff left Barlow's to join him.

Cassie was too much of a novice to run the company without outside assistance, but she had learnt enough during her months with Miles to recognise the right man for the job when she met him, and while Peter Mason was not in the same league as Miles—indeed, few men were—he had enough of the same qualities and ambitions for her to appoint him managing director. When he had proved himself—which might take a year—she would return to New York.

She had attempted to contain the secret of her charade within the confines of Barlow's, but it had been a futile hope, and the 'popular' dailies had had a field day with the story, even though she had refused to be interviewed as, to his credit, had Miles.

Once the media attention died, and things returned to normal, her employees began to see her as a colleague rather than their boss, particularly as she was as hard-working as they were. Harder in fact. Determined to prove herself, she rarely kept office hours, arriving before everyone else, and often not leaving till late in the evening.

Her hectic schedule left little time for outside interests, other than at weekends, and even then she often took manuscripts home with her to read. She was becoming a workaholic like Miles. As usual when she thought of him her love washed over her with renewed force, and she wondered if she would ever forget him sufficiently to fall for anyone else.

Christmas and New Year were spent with friends and family in New York. It was good to be enveloped in their protective warmth, and it provided her with the haven of security she needed after the turmoil and uncertainty of the past months.

As the day of her return to London drew nearer, her mother couldn't hide her distress.

'I do wish you'd give up this London venture and settle here, Cassie. You're much too tense and thin.'

'I'm slim, not thin,' Cassie protested.

'It's that man who's drawing you back, isn't it?' her mother continued. 'You're hoping he'll miss you as much as you're missing him, and that he'll change his mind about you.'

Cassie shook her head. 'Miles isn't the type to change his mind.'

'Then what *are* you going back for? Sell Barlow's, and write off Miles Gilmour and London as one of life's experiences.'

Cassie was almost persuaded. It was torture at times to live in the same city as the man she loved, yet knowing they were a world apart. But running away was the coward's answer, and, if nothing else, the past months had shown her she had the capacity and strength of character to contribute a great deal to the company she'd inherited.

'I enjoy the work I'm doing, Mom,' she explained. 'But if I find I don't, I promise I'll come back.'

During February and March she realised how unlikely this was. She was becoming more involved in the day to day running of the company, and Peter Mason began to seek her advice, and quite often take it.

'I think you should become joint managing director,' he advised her over a celebratory lunch to mark their acquisition of the Californian bookstore chain, initiated by Miles. 'You are, in everything but name.'

'I'm flattered,' Cassie said truthfully. 'But titles don't bother me.'

'Nevertheless, if your name's on the paper it will give you better clout with authors and agents.'

'Now that's an argument I *do* appreciate!' she grinned. 'But if the day comes when we fight over a decision, remember *you* were the one who appointed me!'

Cassie enjoyed working closely with Peter, and they soon each had their allotted tasks. His forte was the financial and expansion side of the business, while hers was mostly editorial, and together they made a formidable team.

While she still took home manuscripts to read, Cassie didn't work with such frenzy—a sign that she had come to terms with losing Miles, she hoped—and she enrolled on a course of cookery lessons that took up two evenings a week. The dinner she had been forced to buy for Miles because of her ignorance had determined her resolve not to have to resort to similar tactics again. Her culinary prowess would never reach the heights, but she would at least be able to prepare an edible meal.

In the middle of June she plucked up the courage to give a dinner party, and it was a great success. Among the guests were Justin and his new girlfriend, Rowena, a talented literary agent, and when she found herself momentarily alone with him for a moment Cassie nonchalantly asked if he saw anything of Miles.

'I occasionally bump into him at Sarah's. David's bank has backed his new company, as you know, and they've become even more friendly. Sarah's expecting a baby, by the way, and they've asked him to be one of the godparents.'

Perhaps he was one of the parents! Cassie thought wickedly, then dismissed the notion. Neither of them would be that stupid. Miles was too distinctive-looking a man for them to run such a risk.

'I hear he's doing well,' she said. 'The serialisation of Seamus O'Mara's new book on television must have given a boost to the paperback edition.'

'It did. Sarah tells me he's already exceeded the financial target he'd set himself for three years hence! It must have been a blow to you when he left.'

'It was,' she admitted amiably. 'But Peter's doing a great job.'

'So are you.' Justin's eyes ranged over her. 'Rowena says you're brilliant.'

Cassie laughed. 'That's because I recently signed up one of her authors!'

'I know. April Davis. Rowena thinks she'll be a runaway bestseller.'

Cassie nodded, and moved off to take care of her other guests. But later that night, when everyone had gone home and she was leisurely tidying the living-room, she remembered how scathing Miles had been when she had suggested he buy the April Davis book. Raunchy rubbish, he had termed it, but Peter had not had the same qualms, agreeing with her that it had great female appeal, and would sell by the million.

'I think we should assign it a large advertising budget, and see it's out in time for Frankfurt,' he had advised, naming one of the most important trade fairs in the publishing calendar.

Cassie had agreed, and from tomorrow onwards was directing all her energy into the book's promotion.

Inevitably there were conferences with their advertising agency, and in particular Clive Gordon, who handled their account. Inevitably he asked her out, and she accepted. They had mutual interests—and a mutual disinterest in a permanent relationship. Cassie was still too emotionally raw from Miles to think of the long term with another man.

Much to her surprise she found that chat-show hosts were as interested in meeting her as April, and she was invited to be a guest on several programmes.

'Apart from discovering April, which is a story in itself, you're young, beautiful, and immensely rich,' Clive grinned, when she commented on it to him. 'That makes you equally watch-worthy!' He rubbed the side of his chin, a gesture he often made before saying something delicate.

'Out with it,' she said slyly.

'You're too perceptive!'

'Only because you give yourself away.'

'Tell me how.'

'And lose my advantage with you?' Chuckling, she shook her head. 'Come on, what's on your mind?'

'A question. About Miles, actually. Will it worry you to see him at Frankfurt? You haven't spoken to him since he left the company, have you?'

'No. But I'm quite looking forward to it,' she lied. 'I know he's doing well, but so are we. It's taught me that no one is indispensable.'

'You're doing better money-wise,' Clive concurred, 'but you've lost many of your prestigious authors.'

'Temporarily. Once they see we're successful without him, some of them will return to us.'

'He was keen to give me his account,' Clive confided. 'But there might have been a conflict of interests, and I turned it down.'

'I'm sure we spend more too,' Cassie said drily.

Clive had the grace to redden. 'I wasn't suggesting my motives were entirely altruistic!'

He accompanied her to Frankfurt, along with several of Barlow's senior staff, and the hustle and bustle of their hotel reminded her of the atmosphere at the convention in San Diego. The thought of seeing Miles was uppermost in her mind, and she was so tense that she was scared everyone would notice it. But if they did she'd say it was Frankfurt nerves!

Anxious to appear her best, yet also businesslike, she had brought suits to wear each day, and ultra-simple, ultra-smart dresses for the evenings. Miles might have broken her heart, but she'd never give him the satisfaction of knowing it.

As bad luck would have it, his stand was next to theirs, and though it was considerably smaller it created a good deal of interest, particularly from Eastern European buyers, to whom he had given seminars, and was well-known as a consequence.

When Cassie saw him for the first time her heart gave a painful jolt. He was as handsome as she remembered, though thinner, and there were shadows beneath his eyes, giving him a tired look. Hard days, and too many hard nights, she thought sourly, wishing that it detracted from his appeal. But if anything it gave him an extra dimension.

'Hello, Cassie,' he said, with the politeness of a stranger. 'How are you?'

'Fine.' Her voice sounded thin, and she cleared her throat.

'You've every reason to be.' He lifted his hand towards the prominent display of April's book. 'You've proved me wrong. It seems the public *are* willing to forgive and forget. I hear the order figures are fantastic.'

'It's how many the bookstores sell that counts, not how many they order.'

'With the hype you're giving it I don't think you need worry.'

'You make it sound like a dirty word,' she retorted. 'The book is good, and deserves promotion.'

'The book is good and sexy, that's why it's going to be a bestseller,' he said flatly. 'You may try to kid yourself, Cassie, but you can't convince me it's in Barlow's best interests to have it on their list.' His eyes lingered on her. 'I hear you're seeing a lot of Clive. How come? Peter Mason not your type, or isn't the chase as much fun now you're openly the boss?'

'Peter's married,' she said sweetly.

'Of course!' he exclaimed with feigned surprise. 'You're the girl with morals.'

'You ought to put your own house in order before you sneer at others,' she snapped.

'What's that supposed to mean?'

Regretting the box into which she had placed herself, Cassie none the less punched her way out of it. 'You and Sarah. Her car was outside your house the night I flew back from New York after seeing Seamus O'Mara.'

'And you put two and two together and made five!' Expecting anger, she was fazed to see amusement. 'I know you like thinking the worst of me, but for your information David came to see me in Sarah's car, but when he went to leave it refused to start. Rather than wait for the AA, he said he'd get his driver to deal with it the next morning, and then took a cab home.' Raised eyebrows mocked her. 'I hope you're not too disappointed?'

'On the contrary, I'm pleased.' Cassie's voice dripped honey. 'You're not as big a bastard as I thought!'

The flash of silver in the grey eyes told her he was losing his cool, and she waited expectantly for the explosion. But as before he did the unexpected.

'Does that mean we can be friendly enemies, rather than just enemies?' he enquired smoothly. 'We won't be able to avoid each other during the next few days, and it would be pleasant to meet without fear of an icy blast that has nothing to do with the air-conditioning!'

It was an olive branch, however ungenerously proffered, and she forced herself to swallow her hurt and accept it. At least it would make their being on neighbouring stands bearable.

'Hi, Miles. Good to see you.' This from Clive who stepped down from Barlow's stand to join them. 'Are you free to join us for dinner tonight?'

Cassie could have kicked him. Didn't he know this was the last thing she or Miles wanted? Yet, to her surprise, Miles nodded.

'Good idea. What time?'

'Arrange it with Cassie. I'm off to the shops before they close.'

'Let's meet in the dining-room at eight-thirty,' she said when Clive was out of earshot. 'Bring someone with you if you like.'

'I'm not here with a girlfriend, if that's what you want to know.'

Blast him for reading her mind more easily than she could his! 'Don't tell me you've embraced celibacy?' she mocked.

'No—love.'

A knife twisted in her guts. 'Are congratulations in order?'

'No.'

'Don't call us, we'll call you,' she quipped. 'I look forward to reading the announcement.'

They dined in the hotel as arranged, Cassie vibrantly beautiful in a madly understated black crêpe dress that hugged her from top to toe, yet made every male present aware of the shapely body it covered. At least, every male except Miles, for after a polite greeting from a shuttered face he spent most of the evening talking to Clive. Yet he wasn't indifferent to her. She saw it in the clenching of his hands as she inadvertently touched his arm, in the movement of his lower lip as she leaned back in her chair and smoothed her hair, the gesture drawing attention to her full breasts.

Only when coffee was served did he address her directly. 'The food's good here, isn't it? Not as good as Le Gavroche, of course, but then their crayfish and

saffron sauce is unbeatable, and as for their raspberry
soufflé...' Deep grey eyes were lightened by humour as
he raised three fingertips to his lips and blew a kiss in
an exaggerated manner. 'Don't you agree, Cassie?'

'Definitely. What a pity they don't do take-aways!'

'I think one might persuade them to.'

She lowered her lids. Either he had guessed the truth
about the meal, or he had gone to the restaurant since,
and seen the dishes on the menu.

Clive regarded them both quizzically, aware that there
was some kind of joke between them that he was not
party to. But Cassie had no intention of enlightening
him, and, judging from the abrupt change of subject,
neither had Miles.

'How's your new BMW running?' he asked Clive.

There followed a discourse on the merits and faults
of expensive foreign cars, and Cassie listened with half
an ear. Most of her attention was given to Miles, and
wishing they were alone. The urge was strong enough
for her to realise her love for him had not diminished
one iota, making a mockery of her hope of forgetting
him and starting afresh with someone else.

Stifled by the knowledge, she pushed back her chair.
'If you two car-crazy boys will excuse me, I'm going to
bed. I've a raging headache.'

'Can I get you anything for it?' Miles asked instantly.

'No, thanks. I have pills upstairs.'

In her room she undressed but made no effort to go
to bed, knowing that sleep was impossible. From the
corridor she heard the sounds of voices and doors
opening and closing. She allowed her mind to drift, re-
living the months she had spent with Miles, and wondering if things might have turned out differently if she
had told him the truth about herself first, rather than
his finding out for himself. It was a useless exercise. Ifs
and buts were negative thinking. What was done was
done, and there was no way of turning back the clock.

Eventually she rose and took off her dressing-gown.
There were no longer any sounds from the corridor, and

she was just sliding into bed, when there was a tap on the door.

'Who is it?' she called.

'Me—Miles.'

Astonishment held her rigid. 'What do you want?'

'To see if you're all right.'

'Why shouldn't I be?' she called, momentarily forgetting the excuse she had given. 'Oh, my headache,' she corrected swiftly. 'I took some aspirins and it's fine now, thank you.'

'May I come in, then? I'd like to talk to you.'

'It's two o'clock in the morning!'

'It's very important. Please, Cassie.'

His voice conveyed an urgency that made it difficult to refuse, so, slipping on her dressing-gown, Cassie opened the door, moving back quickly to distance herself from him as he came in and shut the door behind him.

He was wearing the formal dark suit and pristine white shirt he had worn at dinner, but the top button was undone and his tie was askew. He was pale and breathing fast, and heat radiated from him as if he had just run a marathon. Never had his sexual magnetism been stronger; never had she felt so vulnerable.

Wrapping herself in the defence of sarcasm, she spoke. 'I hope there's no peeping Tom in the corridor. This is hardly the hour for a business call.'

'It's a personal one.'

He took a step towards her, stopping abruptly as he saw her eyes widen with alarm. Not that Cassie was frightened of him. She had taken lessons in self-defence and could floor him if necessary. But she had no defence against her wayward heart, which was pounding wildly in her chest.

'Couldn't it have waited till morning?' she asked.

'I'd have been a wreck by then. More of a wreck than I feel now.' He ran a hand over his face in an uncharacteristically nervous gesture. 'I've come to——' He cleared his throat. 'I came to ask you to marry me.'

Speechlessly she stared at him.

'I know it must be a shock to you,' he said jerkily, 'but for God's sake say something.'

'Get out! Will that do?'

'Let's say it doesn't surprise me. When I think how I behaved I could cut my throat.'

'Do that, Miles. It will make me happy.'

His face, already pale, lost its remaining colour. 'I know you're hurt and angry, but at least hear me out. I love you, Cassie, and I want to spend the rest of my life showing you how much.'

Cassie had dreamed of such a moment, had prayed for it to become a reality. But now that it had she couldn't believe in it.

'You have a warped sense of humour, Miles, and I don't appreciate the joke. If you want to go to bed with me, why not ask? There's no need to go through the ritual of proposing each time!'

'You think that's all I want—to go to bed with you? I love you. *I love you!*'

She waited, motionless, hardly daring to breathe, waited to come alive, to feel joy, warmth, the delight of knowing she could share her life with Miles.

But she felt nothing. Not one single emotion.

'Cassie, please,' Miles pleaded. 'Don't ruin both our lives because of what I did. I'd give ten years of my life for it not to have happened, but we can't undo the past; we can only carry on from here, and I'm begging you to do so.'

She wished she could, but it was impossible. Until this moment she had never realised how impossible. Funny, she had never imagined it would be. One day Miles will come and tell me he loves me, and that he's sorry for what he did, that had been the one thought that had sustained her these past, bitter months. Yet he had just said exactly that, and she couldn't accept it!

Because he was lying. He had done it once, with great fluency, and he was doing it again. She didn't doubt he wanted her physically; it had been implicit in his behaviour during dinner. But proposing marriage was something else again. Was his company not as successful as everyone imagined? He had several prestigious authors under contract, but Seamus was the only one who sold in serious quantity, and he needed to develop a middle-of-the-road list to supply the bread and butter on which every publishing house sustained itself. A merger with Barlow's would be the quickest way of achieving it, even if he had to marry the boss!

She was on the verge of flinging this at him, when she stopped. How much more denigrating to pretend indifference.

'You're too late, Miles. I'm with Clive.'

'Don't be ridiculous!' His reply was instantaneous.

'It sounds that way, doesn't it?' she agreed, marvelling at her easy tone. 'But it's true. You hurt me terribly, and Clive was a great comfort. If I'd still been a virgin perhaps I——' She stopped as she saw Miles wince, and was fiercely glad she had hurt him. 'Well, I wasn't, thanks to you,' she went on, 'and I sort of drifted into it. It developed from there, and we're both happy with the status quo. To be honest I didn't think I'd get over you, but it's amazing how resilient one is.'

'Yes,' Miles said softly, and without another word walked out.

As the door closed Cassie sank into an armchair, numb with pain. Miles wouldn't return, and if he did her answer would be the same. That was the agonising realisation. Was she being too unforgiving, cutting off her nose to spite her face? That's what Gail would say, and her parents too if she told them the whole story. But what they said wouldn't alter the way *she* felt, and in the final analysis it was her feelings that dictated her actions.

She closed her eyes, envisaging the long, lonely road she had to walk alone. Not forever—she was too much of a realist to think that—but long enough for her to have many regrets.

But better to live with regret than with a man you could not trust.

CHAPTER EIGHTEEN

FIRST thing next morning Cassie asked Clive to come and see her, and with great embarrassment told him she had allowed Miles to believe they were lovers.

Clive accepted the news with considerable aplomb. 'I assume you had good reason?' he remarked.

'Yes. I'd rather not say what it was, but if you—er—well, if you have a current girlfriend——'

'I haven't; so you aren't causing me any problems!'

'Good. But in any case in a few weeks we can pretend it's all over.'

'Pity. I'd prefer it to be all on!'

Her smile was wobbly, and Clive placed an arm around her. 'You're in love with him, aren't you?'

She nodded. 'I don't ever want him to know. I mean it, Clive, so don't try to play matchmaker.'

His narrow, clever face held an unusually tender expression. 'He'll never learn of it from me. You have my word on that, Cassie, and it has nothing to do with my handling of your advertising account!'

She laughed, as he had wanted her to do, and together they set off for their stand at the Fair.

The next few days were not easy for her. With Miles on the adjoining stand it was impossible to avoid him, and it was a constant thorn in her flesh. On the few occasions when they came face to face she made polite conversation, but deliberately avoided dining in the hotel in case he was there.

Clive was only too happy to have her to himself, but after a full day's work talking to foreign publishers and agents she was too exhausted to want anything other than a simple meal and bed—alone! Inevitably he made a pass at her one night in the taxi, but when she firmly rejected him he accepted it with good grace.

'You can't blame me for trying, Cassie. One man can often help you get over another.'

'Not yet awhile,' she said sombrely. 'I enjoy being with you, but I don't want it to go further than that.'

'It isn't easy just being friends with a girl who looks like you, but I'll give it a whirl.'

He was as good as his word, and on their return to London she saw him a couple of times a week. He enjoyed the theatre as much as she did, but their taste in music was totally different. However, he was willing to hear Tosca at Covent Garden, as long as she was prepared to go with him to Ronnie Scott's jazz club!

April Davis's book was a phenomenal success, justifying Cassie's belief in it, and her second manuscript promised to be better. Let Miles put that in his snobbish pipe and smoke it! She hadn't seen him for months, but was no nearer forgetting him, and occasionally debated whether Clive had been right in his assertion that having an affair with one man might help her to forget another. Yet she could not bring herself to do so, abhorring the thought of being touched by anyone other than Miles.

In the May edition of *Harper's* she saw a picture of Miles at the christening of Sarah's and David's baby daughter, and she was unable to resist cutting it out. It was only a small photograph, but better than nothing. She placed it in the top drawer of her dressing-table, and occasionally stole a glance at it. She knew she was prolonging memories of a chapter in her life that was best closed, but didn't have the courage to throw it away.

A visit from her parents was a welcome diversion, and no sooner had they left than she embarked on a fly/drive holiday with Gail and her husband Steve, who was in Europe producing a film.

Their destination was Maaestrazgo, a little-known region of Spain that was almost untouched by tourists and barely touched by the twentieth century. Collecting a car in Barcelona, their first stop was Alcañiz, a small town beside the Rio Guadope, where they stayed for several nights at a Parador, using it as a base to explore the region.

From there they moved on to Tureul, checking in at an isolated riverside hotel, set in countryside that was wild, rocky and virtually uninhabited.

'It's so peaceful I feel I never want to return to civilisation,' Gail informed them as they set off the next morning to visit the town on the other side of the mountain pass.

'That depends whether you regard Los Angeles as civilised!' Cassie joked. 'But I can't imagine you enjoying the quiet life for long.'

Stephen shot an amused glance at his wife. 'One day without a walk down Rodeo Drive and you'd get withdrawal symptoms!'

After a spectacular drive through pine-clad mountains they reached Rubielos de Mora, enclosed within medieval walls and interwoven with narrow cobbled streets. They explored it leisurely, then ate lunch at a seventeenth-century convent which had been converted into a hotel.

'Who's going to drive back?' Gail asked as she sipped her Cava, a champagne-style wine that was a speciality of the region.

'Not you or Steve,' Cassie affirmed, nodding towards the empty bottle husband and wife had shared. 'It had better be me. I've only had one glass.'

'I don't think we're in danger of being breathalysed!' Steve said.

'I was thinking of those hair-raising bends,' Cassie answered.

'By all means drive if it makes you feel happier.'

Cassie did, and before long Steve and Gail had dozed off to sleep, leaving her with her thoughts. As always they turned to Miles, and she wondered what he was doing—and with whom!

She reached the top of the pass along a high plateau, and began the descent to the valley below. As she approached a particularly sharp bend she set her foot on the brakes.

Nothing happened.

She pressed harder, but instead of slowing down the car went faster. The gears were automatic so there was no way of changing down to reduce speed, and she tried the handbrake, warning her friends, who were now wide awake, to prepare for a sharp jolt when they stopped. But whatever had snapped—and she assumed it was the main cable—had affected the handbrake too, and the speedometer crept perilously higher.

'What can we do?' Gail asked in a high voice.

'Pray!' Cassie said grimly, and concentrated on negotiating the next bend, narrower and more twisting than the last. But all was lost as she saw another car approaching her. She pressed the hooter, attempting to warn the driver that she wasn't able to slow down.

To no avail. Seemingly oblivious, he continued relentlessly towards them, and with horror she knew there was only one recourse left to her.

'Hang on tight!' she warned and, twisting the wheel in an effort to avoid a head-on collision and certain death, plunged the car over the side of the road into the rugged terrain below.

Cassie heard someone calling her name, and with a great effort opened her eyes. She was in a flower shop, or possibly a garden in full bloom, for all she saw was roses and carnations. She blinked and moved her head, and a white wall with a window inset in it and cloudless blue sky beyond came into view. She wasn't outside, then. So where was she?

She tried to think, but her brain was too muddled. If she could sit up maybe she would recognise her surroundings. She pressed her hands down to give her leverage, but they had no feeling in them and gave way beneath her, and she fell back with a frightened cry.

'So you are awake, señorita.' The same voice that had called her name spoke again. The English was good, but heavily accented. 'I will help you sit up.'

Strong hands gripped her, and Cassie discerned the white uniform of a nurse.

'Where am I?' she asked in a thin voice barely recognisable as her own. 'What's wrong with me?'

The middle-aged woman patted her hand reassuringly. 'Nothing too terrible. A broken nose—but that has been re-set—a fractured wrist and bruised ribs.'

'How—where?' Cassie struggled to remember, but it was the sudden sound of a car hooter in the street below that jogged her memory and led to total recall. 'My friends! Are they——?'

'They are both well. Better than you, señorita,' the nurse assured her. 'It is a miracle none of you were killed.'

'When can I see them?' Cassie asked, uncertain whether the woman was lying.

'All in good time. Your parents and fiancé are waiting outside, and I will allow them in first.'

'Fiancé?' Cassie wanted to say she didn't have one, but the effort was beyond her. 'My parents... Yes, I want...' Too exhausted to finish, she closed her eyes again, long, thick lashes shading the black and blue swelling below.

The sky was dark when she awoke again, the room lit by the soft glow of a dimmed light. She felt a little better, but was aware of pain in her wrist and face. Tentatively she raised her fingers to her nose, startled to find it covered by a rigid plaster dressing. Of course, it had been broken!

'You're awake. Good.' A figure rose from a seat near the window, and moved towards her. It was the same nurse as before.

'My face feels as if it's had rocks thrown at it.'

'You landed on one when you were thrown from the car,' came the explanation. 'Would you like an injection to ease the pain?'

'No, thank you. It's bearable. But I'd like to see my parents if they are still here.'

'They are in the waiting-room with your fiancé.'

This was the second time the nurse had mentioned him, and she was puzzled as to who it was. Peter Mason? Clive? But why should either of them be here? She wasn't on the critical list.

'I only want my parents,' she said, knowing they would give her the answer.

Anxious faces gave way to happy ones as her mother and father bent to kiss her.

'What a fright you gave us,' her mother said, sitting beside the bed and holding Cassie's hand. 'It's been the worst three days of our lives.'

'Three days!' Cassie exclaimed. 'Was I out for the count that long?'

'Yes. You had concussion, and then they had to op-erate on your nose, which didn't help your recovery,' Luther Elliot informed her. 'Gail and Stephen escaped with scratches, and they're up and about. His film started shooting in Rome yesterday, and he's anxious to get there, but they won't leave till they've seen you.'

'I think you should see them before Miles,' her mother put in. 'Then they can go back to the hotel and pack.'

'Miles!' Cassie struggled to sit up, then fell back with a groan. 'What's *he* doing here? And if he told you he's engaged to me——'

'He didn't. He only said it to the doctors because otherwise they wouldn't have given him any information about you. He was here long before we were, of course. As soon as he learned of your accident he chartered a plane.'

'And a bus-load of flowers!' Luther Elliot said drily.

'How did he find out?'

'From Gail.'

Cassie drew a deep breath. 'Ask her and Steve to come in now, will you, Dad?'

Her parents left, and hard on their heels Gail and her husband walked in.

'What an escape we all had!' her friend burst out. 'We could have been killed!'

'Well, we weren't, so stop dramatising, and tell me why on earth you contacted Miles.'

Gail gazed beseechingly at her husband, and he, sensible man that he was, shook his head.

'You made the call, honey, you do the explaining.'

'Yes, do,' Cassie said gently. 'But be quick because I'm going to murder you in five minutes!'

'I thought you'd be grateful, not angry,' Gail stated indignantly. 'I know you love him, and when I saw you in the ambulance looking as if you were at death's door I thought you'd want to see him before you died!'

'I only had a broken nose and cracked ribs, for heaven's sake!'

'How was I to know that? You looked dreadful. And Miles must have thought the same, for he hasn't left the clinic since he got here—not even to sleep.'

Gail's voice was faint with remembered shock, and Cassie couldn't find it in her heart to be angry. Had she been in her friend's position she might well have acted in the same way.

'What you did was very caring, Gail, and I'm not really angry with you. Now kiss me goodbye, and go off to Rome.'

'We can stick around for another few days and keep you company,' Steve asserted. 'I play a mean game of Scrabble!'

'I bet! But you've more important things to do than win against a sick woman!'

Laughing, they went off, and the nurse popped her head round the door. 'Ready to have your fiancé come in?'

'Yes, please.'

Cassie settled back upon the pillows, and tried to appear as if she hadn't a care in the world—not easy when she was physically battered and mentally bruised.

Momentarily she closed her eyes, and when she opened them again Miles was towering over her.

It was easy to believe he hadn't slept in days, so pale and gaunt was he, with hollows beneath his cheeks, and heavy lines etching either side of his mouth.

'Thank you for the flowers,' she said prosaically. Indeed she was only now taking in the baskets, bowls and vases overflowing with a profusion of morning-picked blooms. 'They're beautiful.'

'You're welcome,' he answered politely, and drew nearer the bed.

He didn't touch her, yet his forceful presence enveloped her and conveyed a feeling of safety and contentment. As she went on watching him she noticed that his expression was still apprehensive, and his lower lip was trembling slightly, which she found curious.

'You look worse than I do,' she said candidly.

'I'm not surprised. You were unconscious for three days, and I was awake worrying over you.'

'Needlessly, as you can see.'

He pulled a chair close to the bed, and sat down. The change in level brought him nearer to her, and her heart thumped like a piston. If she needed any sign that nothing had changed for her she was being given it with a vengeance.

'I hope you aren't angry with me for coming here, but when I got Gail's call nothing could have kept me away.'

His words increased the pounding of Cassie's heart, making her feel slightly nauseous, and sweat erupted on her forehead.

Seeing it, he muttered beneath his breath and got to his feet. 'You aren't strong enough to talk yet. I'll wait until you're better.'

'I don't want to see you again,' she managed to say.

'Hush.' Miles bent and pressed his lips on her brow. 'I love you more than life itself, Cassie, and I'm not giving you up without a fight.'

She was too exhausted to argue with him, and she closed her eyes, keeping them shut until she heard the door click. Only then did she lift her lids. She was alone, and that was the way she wanted it.

CHAPTER NINETEEN

THE next day Cassie felt a little better, and the day after she was more like her old self. With the help of her nurse she tottered round the room before having a bath. She also managed to eat some breakfast, though her appetite was negligible.

'It's the anaesthetic,' her nurse said cheerfully. 'In a few days you'll be ready to eat a horse!' She took the tray, and balanced it on her hip. 'Your parents are waiting to see you.'

'Wh-where is my fiancé?' Cassie asked nervously. Had she really seen Miles, or was he an hallucination?

'He's with them,' came the reply.

'I don't wish to see him. Only my parents.'

'Very well.' The nurse wheeled the bed-table across the bed, and handed her a mirror, a brush, and her make-up bag.

'It's a waste of time,' Cassie grunted, but none the less looked at herself and primped her hair. It was slightly dishevelled and gave her a sensual air that did much to improve her mood. Heck! Every little counted when one's nose was encased in plaster.

'Why not put on some lipstick?' the nurse suggested.

'It's silly to add red to black and blue. My face will resemble an artist's palette!'

'A very beautiful one, though!'

She eyed herself again. Yes, she was still recognisable. Not beautiful, perhaps, but recognisable! In any case, she didn't have to worry how she looked to her parents. But who was she kidding? It was the thought of Miles, who might elect to barge in, that concerned her.

'There's a pile of cards for you to open when you're feeling up to it,' the nurse informed her. 'And a long list of phone messages.'

'Not today, please. Tell me tomorrow.'

'There's no rush. I can make it the day after!' The nurse bustled out, and Cassie forced a smile to her face to greet her parents.

'What are you going to do about Miles?' her father asked with characteristic bluntness. 'Your mother's convinced you love him but won't admit it, and *I* know for a fact that the poor guy's besotted with you.'

Cassie mulled this over. Pride had prevented her telling her parents how cruelly Miles had behaved, but in view of the last few days she owed them a fuller explanation. Besides, pride was unimportant after you had narrowly escaped death.

'He behaved very badly to me,' she whispered. 'Not over Barlow's, but personally. He knew I was attracted to him—loved him—and he pretended he felt the same way. It wasn't until we—until we . . .' She stopped, moistening lips that were dry as dust. 'It was a very cunning seduction,' she finished in a toneless voice.

There was silence in the room. Broken only when Luther Elliot gave a heavy sigh and leaned closer to the girl he regarded as his best-loved daughter.

'Miles isn't the first man to feign love in order to get a woman into bed! It's an age-old trick.'

'That doesn't excuse it!'

'I agree. It's despicable. Any man who does it is a bastard!'

'Then there's nothing more for us to say,' Cassie said huskily.

'Except that it doesn't apply to Miles,' her father stated.

Cassie eyed him wildly. 'You're defending him?'

'Hear me out. And listen with your head, not your heart. Regardless of what he said to you at the time, he wasn't lying. His only lie was to pretend he *didn't* love you. You simply have to look at the way he's carried on

since he's been here to know that. The guy was de-
mented. If he wanted you to think he didn't care for you
he must have had a good reason, and I guess you know
what that was better than I do.'

Everything her father said made sense; in fact she was
staggered she hadn't realised it for herself. And yet...

'Why did he wait until Frankfurt before telling me
how he really felt? If what you say is true, why did he
let us both suffer for months and months?'

'You don't have a monopoly on pride, sweetheart. My
guess is that he waited until he was convinced his new
company was going to be successful and he could come
to you on equal terms.'

'But I'd already offered him a full partnership and a
chance to buy me out!'

'He didn't want you to offer anything. He wanted to
be his own man. Doubly so because he didn't want you
thinking that part of your attraction was Barlow's.'

Tears of weakness flooded Cassie's eyes and trickled
down her face, and her mother rushed forward and
cradled her close.

'Don't cry, darling. Everything will work out fine.'

'The sooner the better,' Luther Elliot added, pushing
back his chair. 'Let's leave our slow-witted daughter to
wipe her tears, powder her plastered nose, and put Miles
out of his misery!'

Determined not to be in bed when she saw him, Cassie
had the nurse help her into her dressing-gown—a very
pretty one with a low, scooped neckline that showed an
enticing expanse of creamy skin—and settled herself into
one of the high-backed armchairs that were popular in
Spain.

Hardly had she arranged her gown flowingly around
her, when he walked in. The haggard man of a few days
ago had gone, and the Miles of old was back—a spring
to his step, a purposeful expression on his face.

'I never thought I'd hear myself say this, but it's great
to see you *out* of bed, Cassie!'

There was amusement in his voice, but it did not reach his eyes. They were dark with concern and gave away his true state of mind. But she deliberately took him at face value, and answered joke for joke.

'Looking like this, I'd feel safe sharing a bed with you!'

'Then you'd be wrong.' There was no humour in evidence now; he was serious and purposeful. 'I didn't only fall for your looks. I love all of you. Your beautiful body and gorgeous face; your sharp mind and sharper tongue; your bossiness, and your inability to cook! And that's why I'm going to marry you as soon as you're well enough to walk up the aisle unassisted.'

'You're taking a lot for granted,' she said, heart pounding like a drum.

'Am I?' He came down on his haunches beside her. 'Don't play games with me, Cassie. Without you nothing is worthwhile.'

'That isn't what you said in San Diego.'

Colour burned in his cheeks, but he faced her squarely. 'I lied. I was furious with you, and I wanted to hurt you. Finding out who you were was such a shock that I no longer saw you. All I saw was Catherine Barlow, who'd played me for a fool. For weeks afterwards I was like a crazy man, and by the time I recovered my senses I didn't have the courage to come to you until I'd proved to you I could be a success without Barlow's.'

He was saying everything her father had said, and she marvelled at Luther's wisdom.

'When you turned me down in Frankfurt,' Miles went on, 'I touched rock-bottom, and I've been there ever since. It wasn't till Gail called me with news of your accident that I realised that, no matter what, I had to make you love me again. And I will,' he vowed, reaching for her hands and clasping them close. 'Even if it takes me years. Clive isn't the man for you—I am. You thought it once and I'll make you think it again. Give me that chance, Cassie.'

Her eyes searched his face, loving the firm features, the well-shaped mouth that had kissed every inch of her. 'You're wasting your time, Miles.'

'No!' He straightened, dropping her hands. 'I'll keep trying for as long as I live.'

'You don't *need* to try,' she chided. 'I've never *stopped* loving you. And I've never been to bed with Clive.'

'Oh, God! Why did you turn me down, then?'

Cassie paused, then decided to be honest. 'I didn't trust you. I thought your company wasn't doing as well as you let everyone believe, and that you——'

'I understand,' he intervened sharply, and turned his back on her.

A long moment passed, and fear snaked through her. If only she had held her tongue! If he walked out on her again, she'd die.

Suddenly Miles swung round. 'I don't blame you for doubting me. I had behaved like a swine, and you thought I'd do it again. But my company is growing so fast it's incredible. It's not as big as Barlow's yet, but a couple of years from now it will be.' Gently he bent and placed his arms around her. Drawing her to her feet, he steadied her until he sat down and eased her on to his lap. 'I really messed things up between us, didn't I?' he said, burying his face into her hair. 'But don't doubt me again. I can't bear it if you do.'

She did not answer and, as if aware of the tension inside her, he raised his head and stared deep into her eyes.

'We're going to be honest with each other, Cassie. Remember?'

'It's Sarah,' she confessed. 'When did you stop loving her?'

'Long before she met David. But I felt guilty because she had given up her career for me, and I was plucking up my courage to tell her I wanted out when David came on the scene.'

'She as good as told me you were still in love with her,' Cassie said indignantly. 'You've no idea how jealous she made me feel.'

'Oh, yes I have. I felt the same over Justin and Clive.'

'We've been a couple of fools.' Her arms came around him, holding his body close. 'I've been terribly unhappy without you, Miles. I never want to be apart from you again.'

'You won't have to be. Your doctor is removing the cast from your nose tomorrow, and then you'll be able to fly home and set the date for our wedding.'

Cassie shivered with pleasure, and rested her head on his shoulder. 'I won't marry you while my face is swollen. I want to be a beautiful bride for you.'

'How long will you keep me waiting?' he growled, nuzzling the side of her neck.

'I won't. What's one thing got to do with another?'

He chuckled. 'When I think of all the times you turned me down, you wretch!'

'I'm sorry.' Desire slurred her words. 'I want you so much, Miles.'

'Then we'd better cold shower together! I won't trust myself with you until your ribs have healed.'

'Can't we at least kiss?'

'I don't see why not.'

His mouth moved softly over hers, his teeth gently nipping the skin. Her lips parted, and his tongue penetrated the warm depth, sliding along hers in a gesture reminiscent of the most intimate one of all. Her breasts swelled, her nipples straining at the soft fabric of her négligé. He felt their pressure against his chest, and his body hardened in response, his tongue driving deeper as he drained the sweet moisture.

Her fingers splayed upon his chest, then moved down to touch a firm thigh. Muscles tensed beneath her hand and she stroked them rhythmically, until he muttered deep in his throat and pushed her hand away.

'Stop it, Cassie. I can't take any more.' Lifting her up in his arms, he carried her over to the bed and set her down on it, then perched on a chair near by. 'Let's talk; it's safer.'

Aware of her power over him, she was content. 'I shall live in your house in Hampstead, and only work part-time.'

'You won't be required to do any domestic chores, darling; you can work full-time if you wish.'

'I don't. I'll be too busy having our four children.'

Miles lunged towards her, then drew back hurriedly. 'Dammit, Cassie, you certainly choose your moments. If you aren't careful we'll be starting number one right here!'

She giggled, then let fire another broadside. 'I'd also like you to amalgamate your firm with mine. I don't want us to be rivals in *any* way.'

'We won't be. We aim at different markets.'

His tone brooked no argument, and she gave in, appreciating why he wished to go it alone, and confident that some time in the future he would accede to her wish. After the first baby, perhaps!

'What are you plotting now?' he asked tenderly.

'Our family.'

'I like the sound of that. But would you object if I had you to myself for the first year?'

'I'd object if you didn't!'

Laughing, he moved over to her, and gathered her close again. 'I've a feeling you're always going to have the last word.'

'Yes.'

'That's the one word I'm delighted for you to have!'

HARLEQUIN ✦ PRESENTS®

A Year
DOWN UNDER

In 1993, Harlequin Presents celebrates the land down under. In April, let us take you to Queensland, Australia, in A DANGEROUS LOVER by Lindsay Armstrong, Harlequin Presents #1546.

Verity Wood usually manages her temperamental boss, Brad Morris, with a fair amount of success. At least she *had* until Brad decides to change the rules of their relationship. But Verity's a widow with a small child—the last thing she needs, or wants, is a dangerous lover!

Share the adventure—and the romance—
of A Year Down Under!

Available this month in
A YEAR DOWN UNDER

THE GOLDEN MASK
by Robyn Donald
Harlequin Presents #1537
Wherever Harlequin books are sold.   YDU-M

Where do you find hot Texas nights, smooth Texas charm and dangerously sexy cowboys?

COWBOYS AND CABERNET

Raise a glass—Texas style!

Tyler McKinney is out to prove a Texas ranch is the perfect place for a vineyard. Vintner Ruth Holden thinks Tyler is too stubborn, too impatient, too...Texas. And far too difficult to resist!

CRYSTAL CREEK reverberates with the exciting rhythm of Texas. Each story features the rugged individuals who live and love in the Lone Star State. And each one ends with the same invitation...

Y'ALL COME BACK...REAL SOON!

Don't miss *COWBOYS AND CABERNET* by Margot Dalton. Available in April wherever Harlequin books are sold.